Her First
Long Length

by
Carbaretta Bartland

Her First Long Length

by Carbaretta Bartland

Fanybedwell Press
The Old Rectory
Cockshute Lane
Bell End
Worcestershire
WR69 4BJ

Whether you're only up for a quick touch or can handle the full extent, Carbaretta salutes you…

Sally Tuggin had been here before. Correction: Sally Tuggin had been here almost every week for ten years, but for the occasional evening when a pressing prior engagement with her bottle of Plantur caffeine shampoo had taken precedence. For most of those ten years, the experience of bell-ringing in Frotting St James had been like watching the Greenland ice sheet melt: it was scientifically proven to be happening but you really couldn't detect any noticeable development from one day to the next. However, now that Sally had finally resolved to grab the tenor by the tail end and shake things up once and for all, things would be different.

Yes, Frotting may previously have existed in its own little bubble, hermetically sealed from advances in ringing, but now, it was poised to take a quantum leap into the brave new world of post-COVID ringing.

Where had it all started, this wondrous revolution, of which Frotting was soon to be a part? Sally tried to remember, but it had all been such a whirlwind out there that she could scarcely believe it at all. Perhaps it was the global lockdown itself that triggered the new universal obsession with bell-ringing: all of those A-list celebrities stuck indoors in their Hollywood mansions with nothing to do. What else could they do but turn to the comforts of Ringing Room and Handbell Stadium in an effort to reach out and connect?

A trickle at first: Gwyneth Paltrow tweeting about her first Ringing Room quarter of Plain Bob, and apologising for her conscious uncoupling of the wi-fi router half-way through the first attempt when things just went that little bit too crackly and pixelated. Then a veritable flood as the rest of the world's glitterati caught on. By the time the virus had been fully obliterated by the hand gel of history, and towers were getting used to the 'new new normal' - or the 'old normal', depending on how you looked at it - anyone who was anyone was ringing as if it held the secret to eternal youth and immeasurable fame.

The Jenner-Kardashian dynasty had been among the first to take ringing really seriously and bring its delights to an entirely new audience. They had ART teachers flown into LAX in private jets to teach them, and they practised day-in, day-out throughout the Los Angeles lockdown on the family's very own diamond-encrusted ring (sponsored by Maybelline). With the benefit of round-the-clock expert coaching, they picked up the rudiments in record time, and it wasn't long before they were able to broadcast the fruits of their labours to 28.9 million Instagram Live viewers:

Los Angeles & District Association
1280 Kenninghall Surprise Major
24895 Long Valley Road, Hidden Hills, CA
Thursday, 21 October 2021 in 46m (6–0–3 in F♯)

1	Kris Jenner
2	Khloé Kardashian
3	Kourtney Kardashian
4	Kim Kardashian West
5	Kendall Jenner
6	Kylie Jenner
7	Kanye West
8	Caitlyn Jenner (c)

Rung for love and world peace in association with Maybelline, and because it begins with K.

With this achievement in the bag, the world's most glamorous family was well and truly hooked. They flooded their social media with photos of themselves pouting next to sallies that matched their lipstick, and Khloé even launched her own range of flattering day-glo lycra ringing bras, which offered uplift, separation and rock-solid support, even when dodging! Kim, however, settled on a more focused approach, shying away from the media limelight for a while to teach herself how to write methods. She took to it like a duck to water, showing a particular fascination with devising new pieces for twelve bells, the culmination of which was the unveiling of her spectacular Gluteus Maximus at New York Trinity (in association with Maybelline).

And so, the stage was set for a furious rush of other celebrities seeking to emulate the most influential media icons the universe has ever known. Bells rang out at their weddings throughout California, some of them specifically installed for the occasion, and *Hello!* Magazine started to devote more column inches to the quality of the rounds and call changes than they did to the bride's dress and figure. And it didn't stop there; it even became fashionable to have bells rung for divorces, half-muffled or *au naturel* depending on the circumstances.

Over in the UK, the Beckhams caught the bug, of course, buying Quex Park outright for an undisclosed figure so that Waterloo Tower could be kept for their own private pleasure. The paparazzi had a field day, hiding in the hedges to spy on all of the usual suspects, as they turned up in dark glasses to make up the numbers for assorted quarters of Stedman and the like: Cheryl Cole, Harry Styles, Kate Moss, Gemma Collins… You name it, they were there, wanting a piece of the action. Madonna was even spotted on one occasion, hobbling from the limousine to the tower door with a bottle of liquid chalk in hand, but that was only because Meryl Streep had dropped out of a Celebrity Ladies' Guild tower grab set up by Joan Collins.

Meanwhile, the media had gone into a frenzy of rumour and supposition that the original cast of *Friends* might even be ringing together. They had all been seen in and around Portsmouth Cathedral on a Guild open day, looking and acting suspiciously like ringers. Jennifer Aniston and Courtney Cox-Arquette, both wearing sensibly flat shoes, had been photographed reading the peal notices in a copy of *Ringing World* at the foot of the tower staircase. Matthew Perry and Lisa Kudrow stood by the font squeezing blobs of glycerine cream into each other's hands. David Schwimmer sat on a pew nearby, nodding his head from side to side in a syncopated rhythm whilst staring at a blue line on his iPhone, and fashion columnists had been noting with interest for a while now that Matt Le Blanc seemed to prefer a significantly longer style of T-shirt. Some weeks later, the speculation hit fever pitch that there was a quarter or even a full peal on the cards, when thieves broke into Warner Brothers and came away with, amongst other things, the title page of a script bearing the words: *The One Where Monica Swapped with Joey at the Half-Lead and Chandler Burst into Tears.*

Of course, the biggest influence that all of this celebrity furore had was upon the younger generation, who were beating a path to their nearest tower to sign up and get involved, forming queues as far as the eye could see and screaming with overexcitement whenever one of the regular ringers turned up for practice night. (*Ringing World* had started publishing *Smash Hits*-style centrefold posters of the nation's must-see doyens of ringing, the ones who had won the National 12-Bell, for example, or who had unbelievably long lengths under their belts. These were the ones that the kids were particularly desperate to swoon in the presence of.) And on Saturdays, when they couldn't ring themselves, the kids would flock to the O2 Arena to scream themselves silly at JLS and Little Mix joining forces for a peal of Single Oxford Bob Triples, or Stormzy's new grime collective doing Cambridge Major on Whitechapel handbells.

Football clubs wanted in on the ringing revolution too, as soon as they realised that the value of their lucrative TV contracts could be substantially inflated through the screening of half-time handbell touches from the middle of the pitch. The fans loved it too, of course, filling stadiums with their rousing chants of 'You'll Never Call Wrong Home'. There were some controversies, though. When it was discovered that the 2022 Association of Ringing Teachers Awards ceremony, hosted by Ant and Dec, was due to clash with the World Cup final, a period of intense negotiation was required. In the end, FIFA agreed that it would be in everybody's best interest for them to reschedule the football for the next day, thus keeping the global media conglomerates and gigantic TV audiences for both events happy.

The worldwide obsession with ringing was ultimately confirmed when 400 million viewers tuned in for 2021's inaugural Eurovision Bong Contest, a striking competition rivalled only by the National 12-Bell for glitz, camp and drama. As predicted, the usual controversies ensued in the voting, when Greece and Cyprus gave each other's hopelessly lumpy rounds and call changes *douze points*, and the ex-Yugoslav countries kept voting for each other's horrific assaults on Plain Bob. Unsurprisingly, the UK finished last with a virtually flawless Belfast Maximus that sadly couldn't compensate for the lingering bad feeling around Brexit. In the end, a band of Spanish air-traffic controllers carried off the trophy with an unexciting but very solid 120 of Grandsire Doubles. They would admittedly never set the world alight for either originality or flair, but nobody could deny that they clearly knew what they were doing when it came to striking.

Boris Johnson and Rishi Sunak need not have

worried about the rate of post-COVID economic recovery: the *Ring Out to Help Out* scheme - half-price peal fees on Mondays, Tuesdays and Wednesdays - got things moving again, and before long, the nation's non-stop obsessive ringing ensured that the bounce-back was swift. Northern industrial wastelands were transformed almost overnight by the opening of new foundries, each one employing thousands of workers toiling round the clock and still struggling to keep up with the demand for new bells. Online ringing influencers helped to bring tourists back to Britain in their droves, most of them now shunning the usual London landmarks in favour of tower grab tours of Hampshire or Suffolk in open-top buses.

New Saturday evening primetime reality programmes such as *Come Chime With Me* and *Four in a Band* helped to revitalise flagging terrestrial TV revenues, whilst over on Netflix, a warts-and-all docusoap explored the legal wranglings behind Meghan and Harry's attempts to purchase exclusive rights to all future performances of Sussex Royal. Film franchise offshoots completed the picture of an unlikely British cultural renaissance. *The Bourne Complexity*, for example, in which Matt Damon had to remember not only who he was, but who he was doing the five-pull dodge with at the front in order to avert a nuclear catastrophe, completed a clean sweep of Baftas, Golden Globes and Oscars.

All of these developments paved the way for a brighter future in which ringing would be the all-important engine for growth and prosperity and in less than two years, the government's debt had miraculously disappeared!

Yes, it's a much better world out there now thanks to ringing, mused Sally. *But will I ever get Frotting up there amongst the crème de la crème? And if I can, will it bring me back my Bob?*

Sally gazed up at the sky wistfully, hoping that Bob was safe. The tail-end of the Florida hurricane that had been racing over the Atlantic for the past few days was now beginning to show its hand. Purplish bruises spread slowly through the clouds over Wenlock Edge and a keen breeze was grasping at the tree-tops, still heavy with their full summer foliage. The dipping sun was an angry yellow-grey and the smell of ozone in the leaden air was starting to drown out the scent of the farmers' freshly baled hay.

Sally started to wonder if it was a sensible idea to have come to the practice at all, what with the dire weather warnings all over the BBC. But she hadn't rung here for five weeks and was feeling the itch. It would take more than a possibly apocalyptic weather event to dampen her resolve and keep her away. She was British, after all. And more than that, she was a ringer! Ringers didn't give in to hurricanes, just as they didn't give in to global pandemics. They just got on with it, gave Facebook the full lowdown and then thrashed out the whys and wherefores with whoever thought they were hard enough to come and have a go.

The first distant rumbles of thunder resounded clearly, and somewhere over towards Clun, a flash of lightning lit up the tyre-black streaks of nimbostratus. A wide veil of rain hung in front of them, heading this way inexorably, and Sally was pleased that she had put on the better of her two Berghaus jackets. *The drive home will be interesting,* she thought, and once again her mind turned to Bob out there in the world somewhere. Was the storm bearing down on him right this very moment? Oh, she couldn't stand the thought of it! Why couldn't she have him back here, now this minute, safely ensconced in her yearning embrace? How much longer would she have to wait for her Bob?

"For God's sake, Muriel!" yelled Derek. "I've lost track of how long you've been trying to master this. Just grip it properly and pull!"

Sally smiled wryly to herself, almost comforted to hear the same old tortured litany from Derek Beavis, which, if you turned up at St James the Dismembered at 7:20 pm on a Tuesday evening, would form the prelude for the weekly practice. On witnessing Muriel Struckett-Baddeley having her weekly handling lesson, ringing visitors would be forgiven for thinking that she was a 'beginner', but she had in fact been on the Brown Pathway for nigh on a decade now and had little prospect of ever getting to Blue, let alone Red. She was making a good fist of it, nobody could deny that, but she was clearly never going to get there. Surprise Major would be but an impossible dream, and she would forever have to look on enviously from the sidelines, as those more flexible in body and mind got to indulge themselves in the delights of Yellow.

"I'm trying, Derek!" Muriel blurted, almost sobbing with frustration. "Believe me, I am! But we've just had the whole of August off and I've gone backwards. I was happy with the Treble, but I just can't see me ever getting to grips with something this big!" She started to let it drop again and the rope proceeded to flop around rhythmically above her head, mirroring the slack slap of her substantial batwings. "These new ropes you had put on in June don't help either. These big thick sallies. They may feel nice to the touch, but the girth is playing havoc with my osteoarthritis." It was no use. She couldn't handle it. She would have to give up and try again another day.

"Five is hardly big, Muriel," explained Derek, calming to a more conciliatory tone as the bell dropped down into a chimeless, gentle sway. "The Treble at Worcester is heavier than that, and this is just our Fourth. If you can't deal with five hundredweight, however thick the sally is, there's no way you'll be able to go and ring up with the Ladies' Guild on the Autumn cathedral tour. Some of those women can handle some absolute whoppers without batting an eyelid. You should have seen Bev deal with the tenor at Leominster the other week. Twenty-two hundredweight and she'd have had it up in ten strokes if I hadn't slowed her down." (*"Take your time, Bev!"* Derek recalled having told her as she hauled on the rope like a navvy at the dockside. *"Ringing up should be a slow and steady pleasure, not a race to the finishing line."*)

"Well, you can't really expect me to compete with

Bev, can you?" said Muriel, with a tone of mild irritation in her voice as she readjusted her bra straps and tucked the ill-advised sleeveless chiffon blouse back into her elastically-challenged leggings. "Bev's been in with the Worcester crowd for years. She's bound to like it big and heavy."

Try as she might, Muriel just couldn't bring herself to like Bev Belleau. Ever since she had turned up for the first time one Tuesday evening practice last October, Muriel just knew that Bev meant trouble. "Who is she?" thought Muriel in thinly veiled outrage. "Who is she?! What is she doing here in Frotting St James of all places?" Bev was down in the Guild's annual report as a member of Granser-on-Severn, which, being a proper town, had a much better tower and more talented ringers than St James the Dismembered would ever have. However, if rumours were to be believed, she'd stormed out, having been overruled on her plan to give the Granser ringing room a feature wall in a Dulux shade called 'Gaping Wound'. That was Bev all over: desperate to wheedle her way in, make her mark, 'improve things' and ultimately to take over. Muriel was having none of it. To her mind, St James was a quiet village tower with low expectations and even lower ambition, or at least that's how she wanted it to stay. Notwithstanding the quarter peals that Mike organised off his own bat, the St James of Muriel's interpretation should only really strive to be a provider of passable call changes on a Sunday morning. Muriel was central to that provision, never having missed a single Sunday service ring since she started ringing as a retirement hobby in 1999, apart from a three-month lay-off in 2007 when she had had to go into the Princess Royal at Telford for what she delicately referred to amongst friends as a 'minor feminine intervention'. (Muriel was good with words; she had been a boarding-school librarian.) Trebling for Doubles and ringing in for call changes on nothing heavier than the Fourth was as far as Muriel was willing or able to go. As soon as she had mastered ringing up and ringing down in peal, she would have a rightful claim to the Brown Pathway honours and would then regard her twenty-year mission to become a ringer as complete.

No, Bev would not be painting these walls with her Gaping Wound, that was for sure. The stalwarts of St James - Phyllis, Veronica, Hazel, Derek, Mike and Muriel herself - would make quite sure of that. There was an inkling of concern at the back of Muriel's mind that the younger generation - Crispin, Sally and Dominic, Granser's new organist, who had started coming recently - might side with Bev, what with her regular gushings about the 'wonderful Surprise Minor' that was the speciality of Granser-on-Severn. Having burnt her bridges with the Granser in-crowd, she was clearly looking to bring her treble-bobbing nonsense to Frotting St James and infect everyone with the dreaded splicing bug. Worse still, they only had six bells at Granser-on-Severn, so now that Bev had got her claws into St James' charming, if rather unwieldy, eight, she would be pushing for Triples and Major all the time. Word would then spread all over that bloody internet thing, and that would bring in all of these new hordes of trendy young ringers with their blue hair, tattooed necks and pierced brosnans. And the knock-on effect of that would see Muriel back on the bench for most of the evening. This had to be prevented at all costs. If progress was to come to St James, it would be over her dead body!

"Hello-o!" chimed Muriel, as Sally squeaked open the awkwardly narrow oak door that gave onto the ringing room. "How lovely to see you back again. We'd been rather worried when you didn't show up for the final practice before the August break." (That particular week had been one of Sally's Tuesdays when pampering had to take precedence over Plain Bob. She had been unable to contemplate dragging herself to the final practice of the season, what with its traditional culmination in a dire bring-and-share party, at which everyone had to pretend to enjoy Veronica's avocado and sturgeon tartlets, as well as Muriel's truly revolting warm prawn horns, the recipe for which she delighted in retelling, whether you had inquired about it or not, which you invariably hadn't. Sally decided instead to stay and home and go the whole hog by experimenting with something reddish in the Garnier Nutrisse range. She then spent the whole of August regretting it and frantically washing it back out again. Only now that she was sure that she did not resemble one of the prostitutes that hung around the back of the Aldi car park in Granser, did she dare to venture back into the outside world again.) Muriel was clearly relieved at Sally's early arrival. It meant that Derek would notice that time was ticking on, stop hassling her and just get it up by himself. Either that, or he would ask Sally to do it for him instead.

Derek, Sally noticed, had clearly come directly from his little annual ringing summer school, as he had had no time to change out of his uniform. For all of his 86 years, he looked surprisingly dapper and boyish in his knee-length grey shorts, his maroon and gold blazer and his matching striped tie. The cap finished off his ensemble and Sally could instantly imagine how he might have looked as a wartime evacuee, standing on a platform somewhere with his leather suitcase, label round his neck, drooling over the arrival of the steam engine that was to whisk him away to safety.

"Evening, Sally! You made it ahead of the storm, I see. Good girl!"

"Hmm, it's not far off now," Sally replied. "I hope everyone gets here before the deluge starts. Oh, how was the summer school?" she continued, indicating with a nod up and down that she had put two and two together in regard to his outfit. "In Kent, this year, wasn't it? You do so enjoy your little annual jaunt with the Society of Ancient College Youths, don't you?"

"Yes, indeed. For my sins…" replied Derek, who was usually keen to witter on about it all in a non-stop gush of child-like enthusiasm, but Sally noted that something about him was somewhat subdued this time round.

SACY was founded in the early nineteenth century by the celebrated doyen of change ringing, Arthur Corser-Painswick. It was dedicated to the improvement of those ringers aged eighty and above who still had a sprightly eagerness to learn. The participants quite literally went back to school to relive their halcyon days of innocence and inexperience: a week of intensive theory and practice, perfectly arranged within a comforting framework of dormitory beds, sugary tea and spotted dick and custard.

Every year, Derek got himself worked up into a real lather of excitement in the weeks ahead of his trip, getting packed way earlier than necessary and making sure his uniform was in tip-top condition. Sally could visualise him being dropped off at the station by Mrs Beavis, ready for the journey with his jam sandwiches and Standard Eight dot-to-dot colouring book, and hurrying along the platform just in time to catch the ten-to-ten to Tenterden. The image of him sitting there, bouncing along on the slow train to Kent whilst revising his methods put her in mind of the age of steam, something that she herself had no real experience of, save for the occasional go on the Severn Valley Railway. She envied him in a strange way, and looked forward to a distant time when she too would qualify to become an Ancient Youth. But little was Sally to know that this year's trip had not been one that Derek would be keen to remember...

All SACY members were expected not only to take part in ringing during the summer school, but also to compose and conduct something refreshing, challenging and original. Derek usually played it relatively safe and chose some trivial variation of Cambridge or whatever. This year, however, he had decided to really push the boat out. It had all been going swimmingly for the first two hours, by all accounts, but quite out of nowhere - and nobody could work out how or why - Derek lost control of his Dickford Water Surprise and it completely fired out within seconds in a terribly disappointing damp squib. Everyone had been terribly sympathetic, of course, telling him not to worry, it could happen to anybody, and so on. However, not even lashings of Eve Strekston's famously creamy bedtime cocoa could lift his spirits, and so Derek turned in early and did his best to sleep off the embarrassment.

"It was a bit of a long way to go, to be honest, Sally. At my age, you understand. Not sure I'll make it next year. Isle of Man, of all places!" Sally nodded with understanding and placed her hand gently on his shoulder to give him a tender pat. "Let go now, Muriel," said Derek, seizing the timely opportunity to change the subject before Sally probed any further. His pupil's pathetic flailing of the rope was starting to look more likely to result in a fatal garrotting incident than the successful raising of the bell. "We're clearly on a hiding to nothing with this. Grip and wrist action, Muriel. Grip and wrist action. That's your homework. I'm going to have to be much firmer from now on!"

"Yes, Derek," mumbled Muriel like a naughty schoolgirl. Ironic, given that he was the one in the uniform, whilst she looked more like a geography supply teacher who had been blindfolded and given thirty seconds to pick out her outfit at a village hall jumble sale. She knew that she had been slack, but the stress of having to help Sue Edge with getting assorted primary school children to Guess the Length of the Cucumber at the Frotting Family Fun Day had taken its toll, and ultimately brought on a spot of Irritable Bowel. She had been far too busy hanging around within dashing distance of the bathroom all week to think about her lacklustre bell-handling. Quite frankly, ringing could jolly well take a back seat.

"Show her how it's done, Sally," commanded Derek, and with a silent nod, Sally took three coils and got to work. My word, it felt smooth! She almost felt as if she was in another tower altogether. Hazel must have scraped out all the old discharge and really gone to town with the Duckhams Hypergrade during the summer recess, Sally reasoned. It even sounded lovely, much less tinny than usual and none of the usual rope noise. *Mental note to buy Hazel a pint!* she thought to herself.

"That's the ticket! See how easily she's getting it up, Muriel? It's all in the wrists, as I told you. All in the wrists." Derek beamed with pride, recalling Sally's very first lesson. She had stood there, a picture of innocence, trembling with trepidation in her floral summer dress and Mary Janes. But, by God, she knew what she was doing. It was instinct. Or could it have been pure, blind trust? Yes, that was it. Derek and Sally had formed an instant psychic connection. The moment that she touched the tail end, she visibly shifted from self-consciousness to spunk under his steely, confidence-inspiring gaze. *I'll have this one plain hunting before the summer's out*, Derek remembered thinking at the time… *and I'll have her inside by Christmas.*

Muriel looked on in bafflement and envy. How was it that certain people could get it up for Derek without batting an eyelid, and yet for her, it kept flapping around uncomfortably around the hole and just never fully got there? She'd watched herself doing it in the mirror and was convinced that her posture and general arm action were not to blame. It was just this perennial problem of the wrists that she had to work on. But how? Could it have been Derek's instruction that was not getting through to her? Yes, maybe that was it. What about that nice chap over in Droitwich, who was always happy to take an improver under his wing with a view to some focused work on handling? Yes, she would have to get in touch and give him a try. He had spent a couple of hours working on Veronica last spring and she had come out of it a changed woman. Much more confident all round, and her Reverse Canterbury Pleasure Place had been seriously tidied up, particularly on the places down.

But, to be fair, neither Muriel nor Veronica were anywhere near being in the same league as Sally, and whatever Derek had put into her way back when, it could only ever have formed a very small influence upon the overall development of a largely self-made ringing natural. Sally *had* it. That was all there was to it.

Sally dealt with the task in hand in fewer than ten steady, regular strokes, whilst Derek looked on in warm satisfaction. She stood it with delicate precision, rising ever so slightly onto her tiptoes to let it sneak over the balance.

"See, Muriel?" said Derek. "That's the way to do it. See how Sally knows exactly where to put her hands?

She grips it in exactly the right spot every time, and up it goes, just like that!" Sally smiled shyly and lowered her gaze, embarrassed by the unnecessary attention. "Thanks, Sally. We'll wait for everyone else to come before getting the others up. That should give you a few minutes to have another look at that Cuntastorp Delight of yours."

Unfolding her crib sheet, Sally took herself over to the bench alongside the balcony and sat down to gaze out into the wide open body of the church. The last of the twilight was glimmering softly through the stained-glass windows and the hollowness of the space before her reminded her of her own soul. With one single lonely tear forming in the corner of her eye, she drifted off into daydreams sweeter than one of Phyllis' village hall cups of tea with two Canderels and a pink wafer for dunking.

Three years earlier...

Sally had never known a more perfect April day. The Cooktown orchids were in full bloom, opening their purple lips to the buttery sun, which peeked out from sheepish clouds onto the rolling Shropshire countryside. She had grabbed Cound. She had grabbed Worfield. She had even grabbed Chetton, having twisted the church warden's arm with a solemn promise to park with consideration. But now for the pièce de résistance: she was finally about to grab Willey! (She had been secretly hoping to squeeze in Tong as well, given that they had had to pull out of Acton Burnell due to a suspected crack in one of the clapper shafts. However, given the heaviness of Tong, Bob had thought it best to save that for another time. In his considered opinion, Tong and Willey back to back on the same day would be a bridge too far, especially given the tightness of the schedule in place already.)

Bob had promised that this would be a day to remember and Sally could detect a heightened sense of urgency in him. He was clearly keen that he should not let her down, and he had worked so hard on his composition, something that was clear for all to see. As far as Sally was concerned, he had nothing to fear: she had every confidence that his Cockshute would not disappoint...

The Dowager Countess of Blackwell, Lady Boyes, was very protective of Willey. She didn't want all and sundry knowing about it and it was very much there for her own private pleasure. It was not her main estate, of course; she and the Earl had won it a few years back for coming second in one of the monthly bridge tournaments organised by Viscount Byskett. The house was nothing to write home about and the grounds were a real headache. They had been designed in 1773 by Capability Brown's less talented brother, Incompetence, whose technique for creating ornamental lakes involved the ignition of several tonnes of gunpowder at random locations around the landscape. As for the horticultural elements, Incompetence had a particular penchant for ground elder, thistles and Japanese knotweed. The end result was a nightmarish jungle of ugly vegetation interspersed with cavernous sinkholes, but at least it had kept the local yokels busy with scythes, ladders and dredging nets for 250 years.

However, notwithstanding the shortcomings of the place itself, Lady Boyes was delighted to discover that the bells in the Willey estate's beautiful sandstone Regency church had promise and were certainly an improvement on Blackwell's clunky old three. Only the very best ringers were given access to the Willey tower and their activities were strictly regulated. One quarter peal was permitted on the fifth Saturday of the month. No rope fees were payable, naturally, as the Countess hardly wanted to give the impression of being mercenary. As long as her valuable recent acquisition was treated with respect and allowed to shine, she was prepared to grant an exclusive forty-five minute period of public exposure and would sit on her spacious verandah to listen in with pride to what was, in her opinion, the finest ring of six in the country. She had them queuing up to have a go…

"I shall be listening!" crowed the Countess from her bath-chair, accompanied by the yapping of her two geriatric chihuahuas, Gillett and Johnston. Other than these performances, she had very little else to look forward to nowadays, apart, of course, from spending the interest earned from various multimillion-pound legacies on local good causes, countless trays of Cesar with prime cuts of quail in truffle gravy, and Bombay Sapphire. "What's the method?"

"Cockshute, your Ladyship," said Bob nervously, unsure if the Countess was actually a *Ladyship*, a *milady* or a *Ma'am*. *Reverend Mother* even popped into his mind, but he was fairly sure that that was something to do with Catholics, which certainly wouldn't be applicable in this case. The Boyes family had had the majority of mid-Shropshire's Catholics burnt as the show-stopper finale to their 1607 Harvest festival.

"Wonderful!" bellowed The Countess. "The dream of an eventual Cockshute was one of the primary reasons why I had my Willey augmented!" The existing five bells of Willey had been joined by a cracking new treble with a self-lubricating bush just twelve months previously, and, inspired by an unforgettable evening by the fireplace with that lovely young man from Sandbach, she took his advice and also agreed to have all of her ball faces reground. "Best of luck to you all!"

Sally mused a while on that day, a day so wonderful that it even outshone the time that they had rung a peal of Bourne on the fourth of July. Everything had been perfect: the weather, the striking, the Ferrero

Rocher provided by the tower captain in lieu of the more typical Quality Street. (The Countess had personally undertaken the interviews for the Willey Tower Captain and Ringing Master positions, eliminating all candidates who could not provide proof of previous ambassadorial hospitality experience.) And yet Sally's musings were tinged with an unignorable sadness. Grabbing Willey had been the last time that she was truly happy. Oh, how did she let her Bob slip away from her? And when, if ever, would she see him again…?

At that moment, reality made a rude and sudden entrance. Into the ringing room strode Mike Lapper, shaking off his cagoule, and Sally recoiled involuntarily, as one might do when opening a food recycling bin in the middle of a heatwave. It was not that she disliked Mike - he was well-meaning enough, after all - but she couldn't help dreading the prospect of being told how turbulence and air inclusion could be reduced with bottom-fed pouring, resulting in noticeably higher metal quality, or how traditional wrought iron clappers were still arguably preferable to ductile spheroidal graphite cast iron ones. Again. For ten minutes. In a warm, persistent breeze of eggy cabbage.

However, Sally was to be spared the usual precis of this month's *Clapper Bush Enthusiast* editorial and letters page: Mike simply popped his anorak up on his usual hook, flicked on the Dimplex to take the edge off the ringing room chill, and sat down in silence, appearing to be deep in concentration. *Another new method to throw at us, maybe?* thought Sally. But she was wrong…

Mike had been to the surgery to discuss his aching

shoulders. He had assumed it to be just his rotator cuffs playing up again. A scan, however, was to reveal the painful truth. "You have the shoulder joints of a steroid-addled ninety-year-old Bulgarian ex-Olympic discus thrower," explained Dr Hook, gravely. "One more attempt at ringing the Worcester Cathedral tenor and it could be, quite literally, a farewell to arms. Break a stay, and they could very easily go flying up into the rafters in a shower of bloody gristle and tendons."

"You can't be serious," scoffed Mike in incredulity.

"Deadly..." affirmed the unsmiling physician. "Bell-ringing is something that must be undertaken in moderation, and I rather fear that you have been ringing to excess. How many quarter peals are you involved in over the course of a typical week?"

"Two or three," lied Mike defensively. "Never more than four."

"And full peals?"

"Well, this week was exceptional, but…"

"How many?"

"Three." Mike knew full well, of course, that he had done four quarters in and around Halesowen on Monday alone. There had also been full peals on

Tuesday and Wednesday, plus two yesterday either side of a rushed club sandwich and chips in the Kidderminster Wetherspoons. And then there was the one that he had managed to squeeze in quickly between the assorted morning and evensong service ringing sessions on Sunday, but that didn't really count, as it was just Grandsire Triples at Broseley - *tricky bells!* - for one of the relative newbies. But none of this was all that extreme, was it? He wasn't even amongst the top three peal ringers of the year in the Hereford Diocesan Guild, even if he did admittedly hold pole position in the Church Stretton District.

Dr Hook wrote something on his clipboard and Mike could sense that he hadn't been fully believed. For God's sake, though, he was hardly doing long lengths of Bristol Max, was he? He could barely even get a sniff of Royal around South Shropshire, so he couldn't exactly be described as a 'heavy' ringer…

"I want you to read this," said the doctor, fishing a leaflet out of his desk drawer and handing it over without looking up. "Might give you a little bit of food for thought." He paused for a moment to meet Mike's uneasy gaze. "Book in with me again after your holiday and we'll talk further…"

Mike was convinced that there was really nothing wrong. Yes, he had been on edge and sleepless throughout the entire three weeks of his Caribbean cruise with his wife, Angelique, a surprise gift that he had felt obliged to give her in a last-ditch effort to save their marriage. Yes, he had spent most of his time pacing the upper decks, staring at the horizon, unable to escape from a blue line that zig-zagged about in his imaginary field of vision like the ECG blip of a coma patient who just refused to die. And yes, he had been shaking uncontrollably on and off and had lost his sense of taste... But even though the thought had crossed his mind, he decided that it couldn't be COVID-19. He'd had the vaccine two years previously; he was one of the first to get it, in fact, having bitten the bullet and got it done privately. He'd already sold the caravan and used the money to pay for BUPA to put him into a year-long artificially-induced coma immediately after lockdown, so that he didn't have to endure a world without ringing. (Angelique hadn't objected to this plan, as she saw so little of Mike at the best of times, and at least it left her free to put the furniture into storage, let rip with the credit card and the CarpetRight catalogue, and finally refresh her worn-out shag piles.) As far as Mike was concerned, another couple of thousand on a Harley Street vaccination so that he could resume ringing without delay on waking had been a small price to pay, and so, even here on a cruise ship in the middle of the Caribbean, Mike felt confident that COVID was the least of his worries.

But all of these withdrawal symptoms that he was

now experiencing were normal, weren't they? Normal for Mike, at least. He loved bell-ringing and he missed it. That was all there was to it, he concluded. Why ever did he agree to go on a ship without its own bells? Loads of them had lovely light sixes installed these days, and one or two of them even had eights! But Mike had known that the temptation would have been too much and that relations with Angelique would have gone positively Antarctic if he'd gone off for a cheeky bong every time her back was turned.

"You've got a problem," said Angelique flatly in the cabin, not even glancing up from her periodical of choice, *Take A Break* magazine, a ready supply of which could always be found in the ship's kiosk. As for *Ringing World*, they had had a few hundred on board before Mike and Angelique had embarked, but hadn't factored in the unqualified success of the Board's plan to increase the circulation by 30%. All of the ship's copies had therefore been snapped up in no time by those cruisers who, like Mike, were gagging to catch up on all of the hot ringing gossip. If he really had to have his own hard copy, then he'd have to get that couriered to the Bahamas and ferried to the ship by speedboat at a cost of $1500, the purser had explained to him on his second morning on the cruise.

"Or you can borrow the Captain's copy if you like," said the purser, trying to be helpful. "However, he's already filled in the Methodoku and messed up the crossword. Oh, and he's written 'LOL' all over the letters page and drawn curly moustaches and glasses on everyone in the Performance of the Week peal band photo."

"No, it's fine," said Mike, who couldn't bear to see a defaced *Ringing World*. "I'll go online."

And so, Mike contented himself instead with his digital download and with scouring Bellboard every 20 minutes for updates. He also filled his idle moments with posting lengthy responses to queries about such things as the difference between Surprise and Delight on the *Bellringers* Facebook page, the standard one as opposed to *Thick-Skinned*. (Mike found the tone of *Thick-Skinned Bellringers* far too flippant for his liking and, whilst he enjoyed a joke as much as the next man, he really did not have any time for all of the habitual cleverdickery.)

With Angelique wittering on in the background, Mike mused on whether there might be a lost little ring of six somewhere in the Windward Islands or thereabouts, that he could miraculously rediscover and make use of to satisfy his cravings. The Dove website would know, but if he was completely honest with himself, Mike knew that there was no point in looking: if there were any bells within 500 miles of where they were currently berthed, his AlarmBell app would already have alerted him to the fact with a pleasing, gentle buzz in his pocket. He wished he had looked more carefully into the possibility of a cruise that brought in a Singapore stopover, but again, he knew that that was just a hopeless dream: one of his second cousins had once shared a taxi with Freddie Mercury and Larry Grayson in the early 80s, so the homosexual stain on the family's character would surely disqualify Mike from partaking in Singapore Cathedral's enviable ring.

"You're here in one of the most beautiful places on Earth," continued Angelique whilst applying Ambre Solaire to the gaps between her toes, "and all you can think about is playing your bloody bells." Mike winced at Angelique's deliberate use of the inappropriate verb. She knew perfectly well that you don't 'play' bells. He had told her often enough. She always used the wrong terminology on purpose whenever she wanted to really put daggers through his heart. That was her way of getting back at him for the years of marital neglect. Hit him where it hurts…

"When we get back home," she continued, "the first thing you're going to do is call Ringers Anonymous." She flung the crumpled leaflet onto the bed, the one that she had found when putting his favourite ringing jeans into the wash the day before they flew out from Manchester. "And you're going to actually do it, Mike. I've had enough of the excuses. No ifs, no buts. It's me or the bells!" And with that she flounced out onto the balcony, piña colada in hand, to watch Antigua shimmering into view from the starboard side.

Later on the poop deck, Mike finally steeled himself to read the leaflet that had been nestling in amongst the decaying Holt and Pitman crib sheets that lived full time in his back pocket. It was written in the form of a self-diagnosis questionnaire. Mike read each one slowly in turn, answering in his head as honestly as possible.

In the past six months…

Have you tended to ring on your own more than you used to?

What possible reason could there be, thought Mike, *to ever eschew simulation?* The very thought was pretty much anathema to him. How else were you supposed to make progress? The self-built dumb bell in his garage was his pride and joy, and he almost looked forward to the snapping of each rope when it came, regarding it as a badge of honour that he had managed to wear another one out in record time. He had admittedly begun to regret his excessive use of Ringing Room in recent months, though. Pressing the same button repeatedly over the course of five midnight digi-peals in one week had brought on a nagging bout of RSI and there was certainly a bit of tinnitus traceable back to the terrible metallic *ching!* of the digital chime. What else was he supposed to do after Angelique had put on her Estée Lauder Advanced Night Repair Concentrated Recovery Eye Mask and gone to bed, though? Before Ringing Room, the Blue Line and Methodology apps had been his only sources of secret late-night relief, but using them was ultimately a rather lonely affair. At least with Ringing Room, there were other ringers involved, so it wasn't a solo enterprise at all. And he could even do it at 3 am in bed with Australians if he kept the Zoom on mute, and Angelique would be none the wiser! (If she did happen to be woken by the repetitive jerking motion of his key tapping, he could always just tell her he was scratching an itch…)

Have you worried about meeting your friends again the day after a bell-ringing session?

Only Hazel, for fear of automatically strangling her.

Have you spent more time with bell-ringing friends than other kinds of friends?

What other kinds of friends?

Have your friends criticized you for bell-ringing too much?

Friends, no. Enemies, maybe. Angelique popped

momentarily to mind, but Mike sent her to Coventry as fast as her fluffy mules could carry her.

Have you pawned any of your belongings to subsidise your bell-ringing?

Does eBay count? Mike wondered. He was thinking of all of his childhood Meccano, which he had found in the loft last summer and sold as a way of getting extra funding for the registration and development of his very own simulation software, Electrobonger®. The programming for Electrobonger® had been a doddle, relatively speaking, as well as a pleasure, given that it afforded him a means of keeping out of Angelique's way during those awkward hours when he wasn't in the tower and needed access to basic amenities such as food, hot water and a bed. It was the filming and animation that was getting arduous and expensive. Those who had volunteered their time to be filmed as animated ringers needed to be given some kind of payment, and then there were the extra sundry expenses, such as nipping out to Peacocks to buy something baggy for Bev to wear. She had turned up in a pink crop top with 'Bellissima' emblazoned across it in sparkly sequins, which she thought would make quite a good visual pun on screen, but which trivialised it all, as far as Mike was concerned. Furthermore, what with Bev's ample frontwork, there was the risk of certain simulator users - Mike included - being uncomfortably distracted whilst trying to turn in the virtual tenor. Mike got around the embarrassment of getting her to cover up by saying that the sequins were catching in the light and causing a glare on the screen.

Have you been caught out lying about bell-ringing?

Mike immediately thought of the time he was supposed to have been going to B&Q to get a new hanging rail for Angelique's walk-in wardrobe, but being on emergency speed dial for all the tower captains within a fifty-mile radius, he found himself urgently diverted to St Chad's for a peal of Stedman Caters on the heavy ten. He had returned home empty-handed four and a half hours later with the pathetic excuse that the exhaust had fallen off the car. Little did he realise that Angelique had already picked up a phone call from Dick Moss, thanking Mike for helping him out of a sticky hole. The only way that he could get Angelique to start talking to him again was to rip the entire wardrobe out and get Sharps in to do a full bespoke refit.

Have you been in trouble with the police due to your bell-ringing?

Well, they did do a raid on that peal at Ludlow for the Queen's 90th birthday, but that wasn't my fault. I wasn't even calling it.

Have you lost your driving licence as a result of

ringing and driving?

Angelique hid it once, on the weekend of their 30th wedding anniversary, along with his keys. And there was that time that he was stopped on the A458, having been seen swerving around erratically over both carriageways. It was not the effect of any alcohol but rather the work at the back of Lickey End that had seized hold of his concentration and threatened the safety of other road users. Preferring not to explain this to a lay person, he told the officer that he had been batting off a persistent wasp, and, having passed his breathalyser test, he was sent on his way with a verbal warning.

Have you been physically sick after bell-ringing?

A bit of dry heaving after Hazel made his Penistone collapse in the penultimate lead. No bodily fluids lost, save for the flood of bitter tears.

Have you had pains in your stomach after a bell-ringing session?

The dry heaving hurt, certainly, but it was the mind rather than the body that suffered the bigger blow.

Have you had diarrhoea after a bell-ringing session?

Stupid question. The post-peal lamb vindaloo was a

sacred ritual to Mike, without which he would feel as if an essential part was somehow missing. The eventual diarrhoea was similarly subsumed into the process. Peal attempt led to vindaloo; vindaloo led to diarrhoea. That was just the way of things. If it ain't broke, don't fix it.

Have you had any accidents needing hospital treatment after bell-ringing?

When his blisters burst and got infected five days into a full week of Spliced Surprise Major peals on Alderney, there had been talk of an emergency evacuation to the mainland, but he just bandaged them up tightly and fought on gamely through each of the final four attempts, promising to scrub the sallies with alcohol gel prior to departure. In the end, they got all ten peals that they had planned and, a few months later, his 400-word write-up even made it onto the bottom half of page 17 of the *Ringing World*!

Has your spouse ever complained about your bell-ringing?

More to the point: had his spouse ever *not* complained about his bell-ringing? The way she went on, you'd think he was going out for three-day cocaine-fuelled orgies, or something. Who knows: perhaps she would have preferred it if that were the case? The mysteries of the female brain were - and always would be – way beyond Mike's grasp.

Has your spouse tried to stop you from bell-ringing?

If only his bell-ringing had stopped him from having a spouse, thought Mike with a not inconsiderable sense of self-pity. That state of affairs worked beautifully for so many other men of Mike's ilk. Just how had he managed to slip through the net of singledom to wind up where he was, spending every non-ringing moment removing matted cat hair from the mechanisms of Angelique's matching upstairs and downstairs Dysons, and matted Angelique hair from assorted faux-gold plug holes?

Has he/she refused to talk to you because you have been bell-ringing?

Yes, but that's hardly an incentive to cut down, is it?

Has he/she threatened to leave you because of your bell-ringing?

Not only that, which Angelique did on a daily basis, but she had also even gone to the cruel lengths of employing reverse psychology and threatening to 'come along and find out what all the fuss is about'. Mike couldn't quite decide which would be worse: Angelique leaving him or Angelique donning a Hereford Guild polo shirt and turning up to everything like a touchline parent.

Has he/she had to put you to bed after you have been bell-ringing?

The evening after Hazel had made Mike's Penistone fire out, Angelique did provide an unusually tender shoulder to cry on, along with a couple of Valium and a mug of Ovaltine. He did manage to sleep off most of the devastation and, after walking around like a zombie for most of the next day, he still managed to get over to Stanton Lacy to call his beloved Onacock Treble Bob Major for a visiting band of Australians, most of whom he'd originally met via Ringing Room. (Mike considered himself an evangelist for certain lovely but sadly neglected methods. As he told the lovely Darlene from rural Queensland afterwards over coffee at the Ludlow Farm Shop tea room, "If you go through your entire bell-ringing career without ever getting Onacock, you haven't lived." She assured him that it had certainly been an eye-opener and that she would spread the word back home in The Bush.)

Have you shouted at him/her when you have been bell-ringing?

Only over the phone. On questions of knowing Mike's whereabouts and being able to contact him, Angelique was like a dog with a bone. Mike had learnt this the hard way when moving over to his first mobile phone with a vibrate function. Throughout the two hours and 56 minutes of his first peal of Rutland Royal, Mike felt the phone go off in his pocket as often as there were bobs called. Indeed, with an uncanny clairvoyance, Angelique somehow managed to time each of her calls with those of the conductor, such that Mike's strange grimacing and involuntary twitches made the other ringers assume that he had had a sneaky peek at the composition.

Have you injured him/her while or after you have been bell-ringing?

I wish, thought Mike. If he could get her up into the bell chamber, the world would be his oyster… Not even Midsomer Murders could come up with the plot to match what whirled around Mike's mind in his darker moments.

Has he/she refused to have sex with you because of your bell-ringing?

Mike couldn't remember the last time that he had asked, but it was a safe bet that Angelique would not have been forthcoming. It was hard enough getting her to agree to a quick plain course at the best of times, let alone anything fancy.

Have your children tended to avoid you when you have been bell-ringing?

Not applicable: Mike and Angelique had no children, the subject of which being one of the few things on which they were agreed. 'Life-ruiners', they liked to call them - *"Add carpet shampoo and Dettol to the shopping list! My sister's coming round with her life-ruiners on Sunday…"* - so there was no problem with being avoided by children. The closest equivalent in their life was Angelique's Persian cats, and they were bad enough, always coming and sitting on the keyboard pretty much every time he logged on for a quarter peal on Handbell Stadium. However, now that he came to think about it, they *had* been noticeably more standoffish of late, seeming to think of him as a stranger. But who knows what poison she had been feeding their impressionable little minds with, along with their Sheba?

To be totally ostracised by all children in perpetuity would be a blessing, as far as Mike was concerned. He often fantasised of ways to future-proof Frotting and the other towers at which he rang against the little sods: *Have the ropes fixed a foot higher and remove all the boxes. That would be a good start…*

Have you been less able to do your job because of your bell-ringing?

I used to be less able to ring because of my job, thought Mike with a bitter tinge of regret for all of those missed opportunities. What would his peal count look like by now if not for the interminable hamster wheel of pay packets and pension plans? Retirement had thankfully improved things immeasurably and he was now finding his work/bells balance - i.e. 0% work to 100% bells - to be just right. That said, he had spotted an advert from Taylor's in the *Ringing World*, in which they were putting out an urgent call for a new tuner. (Their previous one had gone on a water sports holiday to Japan, and got tragically harpooned by dyslexic sushi fishermen whilst scuba diving off the coast of Yokohama.) Mike was tempted to apply, of course he was, but in his heart of hearts, he knew that time spent physically working with bells would mean less time actually ringing them. Best to put that particular idea to bed, he concluded.

Do you find yourself constantly wondering where your next peal is coming from?

I'd be worried if I didn't! Contemplating a world without peals? It didn't even bear thinking about, and a cold shudder seized his spine like the sickening crunch of a broken stay.

If you have answered YES to most of these questions, you may have a problem.

There it was in black and white. Mike could not deny the truth that lay before him. He was an addict...

Seeing Mike sitting there looking decidedly out of sorts, Sally took pity and wandered over to him with a cheery smile and a heartfelt hello. She couldn't have guessed the real reason for his chagrin, but when he hurriedly folded up the sheets of paper that he had been poring over and stuffed them into his pocket, she was worried that his little project had hit a crisis point.

"So how are you getting on with your Battered Sausage?" asked Sally, showing a friendly interest, as always. "Give us a quick peek. I won't tell!" Project Battered Sausage had been Mike's little brainchild for nearly a year now. Determined to devise his own new set of challenging alternative Major methods, he had scoured through the Composition Library in search of rarely rung ones with which he could inspire ringers who were getting weary of the same old same old. Sally strongly suspected that Cuntastorp Delight had already made the cut, following Mike's insistence that she keep working at it and ready herself for an imminent quarter. But how would he whittle down all of the exciting possible options down to the final selection? Cocking Alliance was surely a *sine qua non*, and the joys of

Fanybedwell cannot have escaped Mike's attention. But she did so hope that he had not overlooked Velvet Bottom, and as for Brown Willy, well, if that were on the cards then, as she had already made known on many an occasion, she would be first in the queue.

"Oh, it's chugging along nicely enough," said Mike, "and those special practices we've been doing have given me some useful pointers. I just hope that everyone can keep putting in the graft with it so that it doesn't fizzle out."

"Oh, but you can count on me, Mike!" said Sally. "I think it's a wonderful idea, and I'm sure we'll make a great success of it. Your Battered Sausage will be the talk of every tower by this time next year, particularly if we can get it into the *Ringing World*."

"I thought we could try and squeeze in a bit of Brown Willy later. I know you've been gagging for it."

"Oh yes, please!"

"But we're going to need a bit of muscle round the back. Do you think Crispin might be ready for it?"

"The tenor?" replied Sally. "Why not? Even if it takes him a while to find his feet with turning it in, he'll at least be happy. The heavier the better for him, so he says… But, I thought you were wanting the tenor, to make the calling easier?"

"Well, that's the problem..." Mike gazed up at Sally, a look of obvious despair in his eyes. "I've been meaning to tell you... I may not be able to ring so much from now on."

"Oh no!" Sally knelt down to be on a comforting level with him. "Angelique been giving you the cold shoulder again, has she?"

"Something along those lines," nodded Mike, wincing at Sally's inadvertent splicing of both sources of his chronic suffering. "But she's not the real issue." Mike crossed his arms to gently squeeze his own shoulders, and Sally immediately understood his pitiful gesture. "Doctor Hook says my body can't take much more. I'm going to have to cut down, put it that way."

"I'm sure it's not the end of the world," said Sally, patting him on the arm, knowing full well that, for Mike at least, it *was* the end of the world. "Even if you need to lay off turning in the tenor for a while, you should be OK on the lighter bells, and everyone used to be so appreciative when you would take the treble to help the learners. It wasn't that long ago that I overheard Veronica saying: 'I do wish I could see Mike hunt again!'"

"But I had so many plans!" wailed Mike. "How will I get my Battered Sausage up and running if I'm not able to put myself inside?"

His eyes dropped in despair and Sally seized the moment. She had been waiting for longer than she could remember to ask him, and now fate had given her the perfect opportunity.

"Why don't you keep training me up, Mike?" she exclaimed excitedly.

"How do you mean?"

"In composition and how to call. Properly, I mean. Like you. We can do it together! Two heads are better than one… I can carry the burden and you can keep an eye on things from the treble, just until you're over the worst of the pain."

"Well…" muttered Mike uneasily. "I'm not sure. My Battered Sausage isn't going to be all that easy to manage. I'll warn you: it's hardly standard…"

"I'm not a standard type of girl, Mike," retorted Sally with a glint in her eye. "You should know that by now…"

Sally looked on and could almost hear the cogs whirring in Mike's head as he contemplated this unexpected turn of events. She knew full well this was something that he felt very close to, and that he would guard it with his life. He was a private person by nature, and it would require a huge effort of will and immeasurable trust before he would be able to open up and share the secrets of his Battered Sausage with somebody else. However, she felt that she was well placed to earn that trust. After all, since Robert had gone away, Sally had consoled herself by throwing all of her spare energies into bell-ringing theory and the mastery thereof.

Every evening, ensconced in her moated grange at Girthsmount Hill, Sally settled down in her pristine embroidered nightdress to write out blue lines by candlelight. With Robert now gone away to who knows where, this was a key part of her evening routine, second only in importance to the needs of her extensive menagerie. The chinchillas, long-haired guinea pigs and Syrian hamsters settled themselves down in their cages, nestled in fluffy wads of shredded paper. The frosted hairy dwarf porcupines, Brandy and Midget, snuggled up together in their favourite cardboard box, Brandy giving out her usual, incessant high-pitched squeaks, whilst Midget grunted away endearingly, trying to get comfortable amid the myriad spikes. Christine the capybara, meanwhile, luxuriated lazily by the glowing hearth.

After inheriting this beautiful but crumbling manor house, how and why she then allowed herself to fill it with quite so many exotic rodents, Sally could not quite remember. If Robert had turned up just a year or two earlier, she might have been able to content herself with just a couple of gerbils and a common degu, but things had gotten out of hand during those long months of Shropshire solitude. To give herself a means of distraction, she had gone off on her mountain bike with her close acquaintance, Mrs Huthole, to volunteer regularly for Archie Jardison at his heavy petting zoo on the outskirts of Yankford. Sally would always agree to take one of Archie's sicklier specimens home for hand-rearing, Mrs Huthole not having quite enough free space at her place to do likewise, and her husband being one to put his foot down where animals were concerned. One thing led to another, of course, and being utterly unable to say no, Sally now found herself responsible for a collection of *Rodentia* whose fame had even spread as far as *Countryfile*. There would even have been a full fifteen-minute report, if John Craven had not been allergic to naked mole rats, so they had sent their loveable weatherman, Seamus Toffeeknocker, to do a brief light-hearted winter weather feature there instead, during which he spent most of his time trying to coax a groundhog out of its hutch. The groundhog emerged very briefly and struggled free from Seamus' unconvincing grasp before managing to cast anything remotely discernible as a shadow. The only conclusion that Seamus could draw, therefore, was that spring was certainly on its way, but that the Met Office website would be a more reliable source of information as to when exactly.

Now Sally sat here in silence studying *Diagrams*, utterly deprived of all human company, but the latest arrival from Granser-on-Severn's Riverside Rescue Centre snoozing in her lap did at least provide her with a new, warm crumb of comfort: she stroked her beaver fondly, marvelling at the softness of its fur, whilst trying to figure out why things always seemed to go slightly awry in the middle of her Kent.

Sally's interest in composing new methods had been growing stronger and stronger ever since that long-distant, fateful night of unending simulation in the tower of St James. Robert had opened her eyes to things that she had never thought even possible. It was such a revelation, that she had had a quiet word with Hazel about borrowing a spare key for the tower, so that she and Robert could come in and practise at all hours. Hazel was most helpful and showed Sally where the spare key lived, behind a bound copy of the Church Stretton District Treasurer's Reports, 1918 to 1975, where it was perfectly safe from chance discovery. And so, Sally and Robert were able to continue their late-night private assignations in the tower unhindered, and they both looked forward with itching impatience to the next time they could meet again for a quick touch.

With the warmth of the fire lulling her off into a state of delightful drowsiness, Sally thought back to the last time she and Robert had met for their secret simulator practice. It was an experience that would be emblazoned on her memory for ever…

It was just as she was making her triumphant final blows in his unexpectedly demanding Tickle Cock Bridge Alliance that he whispered quite out of the blue into her ear: "I'm particularly interested in exploring the possibilities of York hunt."

Unfazed by the distraction, she safely put the touch to bed and stood the bell with her customary finesse, before turning to him for further clarification.

"Oh, it's just me coming up with new ideas, as usual," explained Robert. "I've been thinking about York hunt for some time."

"Go on…" she urged.

"It's based on Plain Hunt, but you go all the way out to the back, lie, point, lie, then down to the front, lead, point, lead and repeat."

"Sounds interesting. Why the name?"

"Oh, it just came to me whilst I was strolling around the Jorvik Viking Centre one day. And York Hunt has rather a nice ring to it, don't you think? I can just visualise whole double-page spreads of the *Ringing World* dedicated to explaining the workings of York Hunt, with diagrams and everything, can't you?"

"Most definitely," said Sally excitedly. "We should collaborate on writing a feature. I've been dying to show the wider ringing fraternity my Fanybong…"

"Oh?" inquired Robert, suitably intrigued.

"Tittybong above, Fanybedwell below, to be precise," she explained. "I've been hammering away at it for a while now. Needs a bit of jiggery-pokery at the lead end, but otherwise it works a treat!"

Robert beamed at her in warm recognition. "Great minds clearly thinking alike," he explained, whipping out his pocket book to show her his handiwork. "Behold my Velvet Willy!"

"Gosh!" gasped Sally, staring in wonder at the beautiful but demanding frontwork. "That looks like a bit of a handful! Brown Willy above, and Velvet Bottom below, if I'm not mistaken?"

"Bingo!" he congratulated her.

"I'd love to have a go at it," Sally purred, and so he duly obliged, entering the place notation into Abel so as to satisfy her insatiable curiosity.

Before long, Sally was bonging away like a true professional, and even an expert would have had difficulty in recognising her as a complete Velvet Willy virgin. That, however, was just the plain course. As soon as Robert threw in a few bobs and singles, it became a whole different kettle of fish. She hardly knew whether she was coming or going, and just had to deal with most of it by instinct.

"I just can't ring it off the seventh for some reason!" Sally had wailed, after messing it up for the third time, the simulated ringers standing their bells and staring back at her in blank disdain.

"Use the fourth, Sally," suggested Robert huskily. "Use the fourth." And that time, as if by magic, it had all just fallen into place…

The following day at Girthsmount Hill, Sally laid on a sumptuous lunch of bite-size avocado quiches, pea and mint falafels, spinach parcels, coriander couscous, balsamic broccoli bites and assorted seasonal crudités, such on-point delicacies having become her area of professional expertise. Indeed, her buffet items had been the talk of the county, thanks to the establishment nearly three years back of her own little foodie start-up enterprise, Granser Caterers. Her ability to get men - and even Shropshire and Herefordshire men at that - to eat vegetarian quiche had earned her a reputation that had spread even as far as Leominster. *"She must be good!"* young mothers had said to each other whilst sorting out their babies' baptismal food arrangements, and so bookings had been coming in pretty much non-stop. This evening's spread laid on for Robert's delectation consisted of leftovers from a wake in Cleobury Mortimer, for which the family had overestimated the level of local grief for the deceased. (The farmer in question had applied for planning permission for affordable houses on so many different parcels of his land over the years, to the chagrin of the local community, that you really would have had to bribe them with something more substantial than avocado quiche to come and pay him their last respects.)

"My word, Little Miss Healthy! That was delicious!" announced Robert, ever the gentleman, skilfully disguising the reality that a sausage roll, or better still, a bit of crispy chicken wouldn't have gone amiss amidst the sea of nice greens. Still, it was a damn sight better than the eels Benedict and jugged liver that Muriel Struckett-Baddeley had doled out the other week in Sue Edge's oak-framed extension for the Frotting church bring-and-share fundraiser lunch.

"Dessert?" asked Sally, arching her eyebrow archly.

"I'm sure I can be persuaded," replied Robert with a glint in his eye.

And in no time at all, Sally was back with a tray,

proffering something wobbly, and once again, green.

"Three lime whip..." she announced, scooping out substantial spoonfuls that slapped and sucked as they came.

"How could I refuse?"

"...with a choice of two different creams," continued Sally, holding out a matching pair of weighty, rounded jugs. "Let me guess… Single, Bob?"

"Single," he nodded, having spotted that the other was whipped and thought that that might be a bridge too far.

"Single," acknowledged Sally as she poured it on. *Bob: single,* she thought to herself, making a mental note to herself to remember his cream preference for next time. As with sugar in coffee and tea, it had become a habit of hers always to memorise her clients' choices. It was one of the little touches that made Granser Caterers a cut above the rest.

Over coffee, Robert and Sally sat on the terrace in Lloyd Loom chairs and gazed down onto the wide green panorama of the Shropshire Hills bathed in sparkling sunlight. There was Wenlock Edge in all its glory, behind it the dark majestic sweep of the Long Mynd, and further still, just over the Welsh border, they could even see Sally's childhood home,

Thrustingho Mill, on the horizon, its white sails turning slowly in the gentle breeze. Down the valley in the near distance, they observed Frotting and Yankford nestling in a purple haze, sheltered from the prevailing westerlies, with Sloley Fealingham and Ewe Lovett perching on exposed ridges either side. Beyond them, finally, Granser's magnificent spire thrust itself up into the cerulean air like a signpost to heaven, and they could just about make out the fabulous golden cock atop it, twinkling proudly.

Sally reached down and picked a single buttery primrose. She twirled it between her fingers like a tiny umbrella, and it brought back a sudden, unexpected memory of Cambridge, of dodging back and forth between idling tourists on her rickety bicycle, trying to remember where she was going. In this state of utmost bliss, Sally slid the primrose into her dewy cleavage and started to transcribe, her red felt-tip tracking out the line of the treble as dictated to her by Robert, who led the way with his reassuring teacherly manner.

"Out to the back and lie, just like regular plain hunt…" he whispered seductively, "…and now point. Lie again. That's it…"

Sally guided the red tip slowly in time with his commands, not daring to make assumptions or leap ahead for fear of sending it in the wrong direction and spoiling a perfectly good piece of graph paper. As she knew all too well from bitter experience, felt-tip took no prisoners; one stroke made too hastily and the whole thing would come to a sticky end.

"...and back down to the front," continued Robert. "Lead... point... lead. Well done!"

Sally smiled up at him with pride, pleased to have got it right the first time.

Robert pointed to her handiwork and traced the line gently with his finger. "So, that's the basic structure of York Hunt. From here, the world's our oyster. Infinite possibilities to explore!"

And so, they spent all morning investigating, taking it in turns with the blue felt-tip to see what they could fit around this new red line. Certain elements of sixth-place Fickleshole seemed to have possibilities, Sally found, and there were parts of Cocking Alliance that slotted in neatly around the back. But it was Robert's beloved Double Norwich that they kept coming back to, and once they had thrown themselves into some serious, concentrated pricking, they found it to be the perfect fit for York Hunt.

"Near!" gasped Sally in ecstasy.

"Full!" groaned Robert in response.

"Far! Oh yes, Robert, far! It's come round!" Sally couldn't quite believe that it had all worked out so beautifully. Her previous solo attempts at designing a new method had nearly always come to nought, with either one bell having to make ludicrously long leads or the whole thing ending up false when inserted into Mike's handy online widget.

"Who would have thought we could fit Double Norwich into York Hunt and end up with something so wonderful," said Robert, as he leant back in satisfaction on his chair and pinched a quick drag from her Sobranie Cocktail. "Even the bobs make sense. All we need now is a name!"

"There's never been a method named after the village..." replied Sally, animatedly.

"Well, there we go then," said Robert, rubbing his hands with glee. "Frotting Alliance!"

"Oh, it's perfect, Bob!" she gasped, rushing towards him to hurl herself into his mighty, statuesque arms. Pressing his lips to hers in a reckless, wild embrace, he grasped her close and quite literally swept her off her feet. She felt weightless, even more completely carried away than the time she broke that stay at Cleobury Mortimer. For a moment, gravity ceased to exist and she was up, up in the heavens, her mind a whirl of impossible imaginings…

Then she came back down to earth and gazed at him. Something was wrong. She saw a tear forming in his eye, a tear that would irrevocably stain this perfect page in the Book of Love.

"What is it?" she asked anxiously.

"Oh, Sally," said Robert, loosening the grip of his perfect scrum-half arms, "see for yourself…"

He handed her a crumpled sheet of paper from his back pocket. Sally unfolded it with a mixture of trepidation and deep arousal, secretly savouring the buttock warmth that still radiated from its creamy smoothness.

"*Notice of call out…*" she read aloud, not fully understanding what the phrase meant. Then, unfolding the top third, she saw an emblem. And underneath it: *Ministry of Defence*. "Bob?" she asked, perplexed.

"Keep reading," he replied gloomily. "All will be explained."

Sally raced through the text with a sense of mounting fear and dread…

I am writing to confirm the British Army's intention to call up all members of the Reservist Ringing Corps to undertake operations in defence of the realm. The call to active duty in support of Operation Downdodge, is compulsory and is hereby required of

Liddell, Bob (Major)

"Major? Operation Downdodge?" Sally was almost speechless with shock. "What does it all mean?"

"I've been meaning to tell you for some time," Bob tried to reassure her, "but so much of my Territorial Army role is top secret, and I never thought that it would come to this."

"Top secret?" whispered Sally nervously.

"Nobody really knows about us. The Reservist Ringers normally just step in on an emergency basis to plug holes in illness-stricken peal bands. We've not been deployed for a couple of years on any serious missions, not since we had to go in and help negotiate the *Ringing World* War III peace deal. But now it looks like we're up for our biggest call of duty to date…"

"Oh?" Sally was agog with intrigue and mounting concern.

"The Co-operative Consortium of Central Church Councils for Change Ringing has set up an internment centre on Lundy for the correction of ringers with suspected militant tendencies: the kind that still ring Rutland, even though they have been specifically told not to; the kind that put their threesomes and simulator quarters on Bellboard; the kind that argue with the conductor in the middle of a peal; the kind that deliberately name new methods after rude-sounding places… that sort of thing. It's the thin end of the wedge that ultimately leads to terrorism, if left unchecked, and which poses a threat to the sanctity of ringing standards, or so think the powers that be."

"So what has this got to do with you?"

"Well, word coming to us from our moles is that they are taking it a bit too far. The latest is that they're only allowing the inmates to focus on one method."

"Which one?"

"Water No.3 Surprise Royal. They force them to ring peals of it, day in day out, and one of the CCCCCCR plants always makes it fire out on purpose in the last lead."

"How awful!"

"And then, to rub salt into the wounds, they wake them up violently at random points in the night with full volume recordings of their lost peals."

"I thought Water torture had been banned years ago…"

"It had," said Robert, nodding sternly, "but the old methods die hard."

"So anybody who fails to follow the CCCCCCR rule book gets hunted down and sent to Lundy for punishment and correction, is that it?" asked Sally.

"In a nutshell," replied Robert. "And it's brutally effective, by all accounts. Remember all of that talk about that local faction, the Granser Extremists, a year or two ago? Well, they're all shadows of their former selves now, just toeing the line and doing the Pickled Egg like everybody else."

"It can't be right to crush individuality and self-expression like that though, can it?"

"No, of course not. The nation must stand up and fight against such totalitarian excesses." Robert paused to imagine the horror that could lurk just around the corner… "If you want a vision of the future, imagine a tail end spanking a human bottom - forever."

"I can hardly bear to think of it," muttered a horrified Sally. "So the Ringing Reservists are sending you in to defend our freedom? Is there to be a full invasion of Lundy? Fighting on the beaches?"

She clung to him, terrified for his safety.

"No, nothing so unsubtle as that. At least not to start with, anyway. The plan is to infiltrate and identify areas of weakness. Just me, on my own, disguised as an inmate."

"How will you do that? This is the CCCCCCR you're dealing with. These people are ruthless! If you get found out…"

"I won't get found out. There's a boat leaving from Weston-super-Mare at 0800 hours next Wednesday. It's being loaded with fans of Pudsey. They're next on the list to have their misguided ideas crushed out of them. I will pretend to be one of them…"

"You? Liking Pudsey? Are you really going to be able to keep up that kind of ludicrous pretence?"

"It's a tall order, I know, but I've been training myself up. I can now completely stifle the involuntary gagging reflex whenever I look at the blue line."

"How long will you be there? I'll be worried sick!"

"Only as long as it takes to find out what kind of atrocities are going on on the island and work out a plan to release the inmates. As soon as we have an invasion strategy in place, a full battalion of Reservist

Ringers will go ashore, followed by a second wave of diehard mercenaries from Facebook *Thick-Skinned Bell Ringers*. It should all be over by Christmas, my darling."

"But how will I know that you are safe?" begged Sally.

"I'll find a way to contact you. The mobile signal on Lundy is unreliable at the best of times, sadly, but the Marisco Tavern has wi-fi, so I'll drop you a WhatsApp when I can, and click Like on your Bellboard performances."

Sally hung her head in sorrow. A tiny crystal tear traced its way down her cheek. It splashed onto one of the sheets of squared paper that still sat in her lap, spoiling the internal places of her Fanybong.

"But what about our Frotting Alliance?" she asked him, staring deep into his soul through welling eyes. "And your Velvet Willy and my Fanybong? All of our wonderful inventions? Will they remain unrung?"

"Sally, my darling..." whispered Bob as he stooped to kiss her just above her shimmering primrose. She smelled, as she so often did, of jasmine. Jasmine, with a faint subtle undertone of coypu.

"Call me like you called me that very first time we

met," she interjected with a coquettish simper, trying her best to be brave.

"Observation?"

"Oh yes, Bob, yes!" she ejaculated. "It makes me feel so young again, so innocent, like I was when a peal was but the stuff of a mad girl's dreams, let alone a whole long length!"

"Well, then, my darling Observation," said Bob every so quietly into her attentively trembling ear, "we will find a way to splice these wonderful inventions, and on a day just like this, we will ring them in triumph. Everyone in the valley will be unforgettably stirred by the exquisite sounds of Frotting, and, what's more..."

"Yes, Bob?"

Robert looked deep into her eyes with absolute sincerity. "What's more, it will be the very first performance on our brand-new bells!"

It all seemed like such a long time ago. This talk of 'we' and 'our brand-new bells'. Sitting here now, contemplating Mike's Battered Sausage and steeling herself for several abortive attempts to tighten up Veronica's Reverse Canterbury Pleasure Place, Sally mused on what might have been.

Sally had longed for a cracking heavy eight for years, way before Robert had ever appeared on the scene, but had always assumed that the church finances would never stretch far enough; she just let her dream bubble away on the back-burner, almost forgotten. Derek Beavis had had it on his development plan since the early noughties, and Hazel, having taken up her grease gun and an array of clamps for a good few hours of in-depth exploration of possibilities, was confident that her solid frame could support a heavier set. All they needed was a quote from Meltham, Downe & Bymore, and then the fundraising could begin in earnest. But nobody had taken it any further until Robert grabbed hold of the reins and willed Sally on to really believe that it could happen. They had planned it all out. It would be wonderful!

But then suddenly all of those plans seemed to have disappeared into the ether. Robert had gone to Lundy and his contact had become less and less frequent. Sally looked at Bellboard every evening to see if he got any of his twice-daily peal attempts of Water No.3 Surprise Royal, but there was always nothing. (God, these people really knew how to break a man! *"Please, God, I can't take it anymore! No more 10ths place lead ends...!"* she could hear them screaming.) She tried to imagine Bob's suffering, tried to take heart from the knowledge that he was doing it for his country, for freedom. But if only he could *communicate* with her a little more, console her in his absence. Send her a slightly out-of-focus photo of the band in the ringing room, maybe. Was that too much to ask?

And as time went on, what's more, the very tone of Robert's fractured WhatsApp correspondence seemed to change. He actually seemed to be becoming one of *them*! He *enjoyed* belittling the genuine likers of Rutland and seemed to revel in witnessing the systematic dismantling of their personalities. Instead of heartfelt messages of love, he was now sending her hyperlinks to CCCCCCR 'Learning and Development' documents and bullet-pointed responses to items on previous years' AGM minutes.

And a horrible thought eventually, and inevitably, crossed her mind. Did Robert love her, or did he love the CCCCCCR? Loving both was an impossibility; that, she instinctively knew. But had they got into his mind so fully and so irrevocably as to push her out forever?

Sally missed the old Bob! Oh, how she missed him! She had particularly fond memories of his Long London, and doubted that she would ever find anyone else who could rival it, the way it worked its magic at the back, always seeming to slot in perfectly around her own immaculately timed fish tails. But the new Bob had other fish to fry, and of this, she had to be accepting.

With this truth in mind, after several long months and no Bob in sight, she revisited the bell project and took it upon herself to make it happen, with or without his involvement. Without new bells, there was no way that Frotting would be able to keep up with the Kardashians, and all of those other beautiful, glamorous Hollywood ringers who could afford to commission the very best bells that money would buy. If nobody did anything about it, the next generation would never come near the place and Frotting would be stuck in the doldrums forever! Sally just could not bear to see that happen. Hazel and Derek would need a bit of chivvying, of course, but if Sally made it clear that she would take charge of the fundraising, then they would surely have no objections.

And fundraise she did, as if her life depended upon it. Granser Caterers formed the backbone of her efforts and she was up at the crack of dawn every Saturday, getting a pop-up bell-fund buffet ready for whichever village hall she had managed to get hold of. It wasn't long before her Three Lime Whip was the talk of the diocese and, little by little, the funds trickled in towards the necessary target of £100,000. Jumble sales, drive-thru car wash mornings in the church car park, choir concerts, rodent-petting workshops… the ideas came thick and fast, and Sally was indefatigable in her drive to get it all organised with military precision and, above all, a focused eye on the profit margins. Everyone else made their own little contribution too, of course. The church porch was transformed almost overnight into a makeshift honesty shop, at which all of the ringers sold whatever they had to offer. Muriel laid out her very own hand-written and illustrated recipe cards; Phyllis offered gallons of lemon curd and assorted fabric-topped jams; and, when the need to let out a bit of pent-up aggression took hold, Mike got busy with his axe to produce a nice regular supply of morning wood at £3 a bundle.

The biggest success, though, was undeniably the mobile belfries festival that Sally had managed to get set up for a glorious weekend in May. With the promise of a spit roast and CAMRA award-winning real ales, she had been able to persuade those in charge of the Lichfield one to hitch it up to the

Transit and bring it over, and the Charmborough Ring had also been booked. Martin Draycott from Market Drayton brought his record-breaking micro-ring, and Brian Farnett had made the considerable trek from Friern Barnet with his light eight. Brian had taken a little more cajoling, as his was the mini-ring that had taken a battering at the fateful festival a couple of years back. After a costly reinforcement procedure, it had, however, lived to see another day, although Brian made it clear that he would no longer be letting it take a pounding from the kind of ham-fisted oafs who had loosened it so badly at Bromsgrove. It would take more than the likes of Old Speckled Hen to make him drag his ring up the M40 on a Saturday morning, he clarified shirtily. However, as soon as Sally mentioned that she had a whole crate of Cornish Knockers, Brian's mood lightened and he confirmed that he was happy to be on board.

On the first morning, things had been looking a bit tight schedule-wise, but aside from some unforeseen erection issues early on due to damp conditions underfoot, all of the exhibitors managed to get them up just in time for the grand opening. Sally breathed a sigh of relief when each ring got the thumbs up and she could start letting in the clamorous throngs who were queuing the whole way round the duck pond. Ringers of all levels had flocked in to test their mettle against these unique mini-rings, including several from deepest, darkest Powys and one even coming down especially all the way from Congleton! They tried their hand at every method imaginable, exploring the positional complexities of operating in such a tight space and getting used to the idiosyncrasies of a more delicate handling technique.

All in all, a great time was had by all, and the donations flooded in, not only in gratitude for the provision of such wonderful rings, but also for the top-notch pork, which went down a treat alongside Sally's substantial summer salads and generously filled baps. In addition, participants splashed out on the various promotional items that were available for sale, such as the ever-popular HDGB nude calendar, and it wasn't long before the various Tupperware tubs that Muriel had brought along in lieu of cash boxes were heavy with coinage and overflowing with lovely, crisp notes. To put the icing on the cake, Lady Boyes made an unannounced appearance towards the end of the Sunday afternoon, having been chauffeured over in the Bentley along with her butler, Gerard, and the ubiquitous chihuahuas.

"I won't stay long," she announced from her bath chair, as Gerard proceeded to give her the royal pushabout, with Gillett and Johnston yapping happily in her tartan-blanketed lap. "I'm having the Bysketts over for Bridge at Blackwell this evening. But I wouldn't want to miss out on such a unique spectacle as this!"

"I hope that you enjoy yourself, Your Ladyship," said Sally. "You can even have a go if you wish. You can remain seated to handle Martin Draycott's micro-ring."

"Bless you, my dear," replied Lady Boyes, patting Sally's hand warmly. "How exciting! I haven't rung since the time of the Cod Wars!" (Lord Boyes' substantial investment in the Icelandic fishing industry in the 1970s boosted the family fortune several times over, but the memory of it all was bittersweet for his wife, who was paralysed from the waist down after slipping on a patch of herring guts outside a Reykjavik fish cannery.) "Strange to think," she mused, "that we have now had over forty years of Cod Peace... But where was I? Oh yes... ringing! What a treat after all this time!"

And so, after Gerard had tricked the dogs onto the ground with a morsel of Wagyu beef and then wheeled her into position, Lady Boyes reached forward to grab hold of Martin Draycott's tiny little One. It felt terribly light, and she feared she might damage it somehow, what with there being so little to hold onto and no stay at all. However, she soon got the hang of the simple cow-milking action that Martin explained to her, and proceeded to plain hunt for him and four others in Plain Bob Doubles as if she'd rung only yesterday. It all just came flooding back and the assembled onlookers could see in her a glimmer of the celebrated young woman who never balked at a prospect of a spliced peal and who seized upon the offer of a long length with both hands.

"Thank you all so much," she squealed in joy as it came round. "I feel quite, quite rejuvenated! I shall treasure the memory of this day forever, and please allow me, dear Sally, to make a donation to the bell fund."

"That's most generous of you, Lady Boyes," said Sally, curtseying, as Her Ladyship snapped her fingers and commanded Gerard to hand over a wedge of unmarked twenties as thick as a brick.

"The pleasure is all mine, my dear, all mine," replied Lady Boyes as she took Sally's hand and clasped it firmly between both of hers. "One small piece of advice, though, if I may…"

"Please go ahead, Your Ladyship," said Sally. "I'm all for a bit of outside input."

"Very well," continued Lady Boyes. "Speaking from experience, my dear, I do find that there is such a thing as *too* well hung."

"Oh, really?" replied Sally with surprise. "Do elaborate."

"You can overegg the pudding, I rather think.

There's nothing wrong with a bit of play around the back end, for example. If your ring has no faults at all, then it lacks character, don't you agree? Takes all the fun out of it if there's nothing there to take you by surprise now and then."

As if on cue, Gillett and Johnston started yapping again, wanting to be in on the conversation, whilst Sally nodded in agreement. She had never really thought of it before, but yes, perhaps a little bit of quirkiness, of unpredictability, was what made for a memorable ring. It certainly made for a memorable man, after all!

"Let us pray that your Robert returns safely in time for the installation and blessing," said Lady Boyes, patting her consent for the chihuahuas to resume their customary position, side by side on her lap.

Sally nodded again, in silence, trying to stem the tide of tears that threatened to breach her defences.

Her mind drifted back to the recurring nightmare that she had of him returning from Lundy, arm in arm with a new love, a carefree young blonde who had never had any difficulty on the Bristol front, and who could take on Brown Willy at the drop of a hat.

"Single?" Bob asked Sally at the climax of the dream, with a tone of vindictive arrogance.

"Single, Bob," confirmed Sally, unable to conceal her bitter contempt, her hysteria mounting with each nail that it hammered in the coffin of her heart. "Single! Single! Single!" And this was the point at which she would always wake up, the dreaded word still echoing in her head: *Single…*

Sally had tried to move on emotionally, of course she had. Initially, she threw herself into developing the status of Granser Caterers within the local food scene, forming alliances with established suppliers. Ludlow Farm Shop, for example, couldn't get enough of her homemade clam sauce, and it soon became a bestseller on their condiment shelves. So, all in all, business was brisk and she was starting to make a real culinary name for herself.

Work was not enough, though, and hobbies became a further means of filling the gigantic hole left by Robert's absence. Mrs Huthole was particularly good at chivvying her on to get involved in new activities, and they always looked forward to their weekly stints of footpath maintenance work on behalf of Shropshire's very own rambling charity, The Stile Gurus. And in the evenings, there were crafting opportunities aplenty. Sally made the most of her Thursdays, for example, by going to *Get Felt!* up at Wetsoap College, taking bagfuls of unwanted guinea pig and beaver hair with her to transform into all manner of fuzzy fabric creations.

However, the elephant in the room remained Sally's

desperate hunger for companionship, for understanding, and yes, for intimacy. Somebody out there must be able to help her out of this impasse of ennui, and if it wasn't to be Robert, then maybe, she concluded regretfully, it might just have to be someone else.

Finally, she had plucked up the courage to put on her sexiest little black dress along with her stylish teal-green HDGB fleece with the embroidered logo and her Ringing Remembers earrings, and took herself off to Granser Singles to dance the night away with whichever available man she could find. There had been a few promising options amongst them - a blond dentist from Bridgnorth called Alexander, a philosophy teacher in trendy baggy jeans called Tom and a tall, dark, handsome car valet called Gary - which made a welcome change from the ringing fraternity, in which single men were virtually non-existent. Why was it, Sally often wondered, that male bell-ringers always had hordes of women after them these days? They virtually had to beat them back with sticks! Sally had gone through a complete mental list of everyone in the Hereford Guild and - apart from Crispin, and maybe Dominic the organist, neither of whom counted for her purposes - she could not think of a single unattached male member. So, a non-ringing dentist, philosophy teacher or car valet it might have to be. Oh well, she could at least get them to try out something different from their usual interests and, if they were feeling brave, she might be able to persuade them into the tower and let them have a go at a bit of ringing up and - who knows? - even a bit of pulling off.

Sadly, though, after the exchange of phone numbers over just one more ice-cold strawberry daiquiri, nothing more had come of Alexander, Tom or Gary. They had disappeared into the unknown outer reaches of the non-ringing world, that parallel universe that was so similar to, and yet so incompatible with her own. No matter how often she gave Granser Singles a go, she just couldn't get the hang of it, and the whole malarkey just gradually trickled away to nothing.

She even tried installing the Ringr app - *Find like-minded ringing companions near you!* - but on those rare occasions that an alert did pop up - *Dong ding!* - she just knew that she didn't stand a chance. Yet another Ryan Reynolds look-alike with granite cheekbones and a washboard six-pack, fresh off the plane from Auckland, looking for love and peal opportunities in the Much Wenlock area... And, lo and behold, moments later the inevitable second alert - *Ding dong!* - along with its sorry little message: *No longer available.*

Eventually, though, she was met with a bit of a blast from the past. The *Dong ding!* chimed whilst she was giving her capybara a long overdue flea treatment...

"Oh my God!" she squeaked to herself in disbelief. *"Little Rob Boyle!"*

There he was, beaming back at her from his blurry profile picture, all five-foot-four of him. The picture appeared to have been taken at Liverpool Cathedral, one of those *'Ooh, look at me, I've rung the big one!'* photos. His message to her said: *"Sally Tuggin? Well, I never! Who would have thought you would ever get into ringing… or be available and looking for love?! What do you ring?"*

Sally was immediately wary and paused before replying. She hadn't seen Little Rob Boyle for years, not since before she started ringing herself. They had been in the same sixth-form college together and, although she did languages and he was maths, DT and economics, they overlapped for general studies, so she got to know him through that. He was alright, she supposed, and she couldn't deny that he had lovely eyes. He told her all about his ringing exploits, before any of it made any sense to her whatsoever, and it sounded, well, boring, but in an interesting kind of way.

Eventually, Sally now recalled, she had succumbed to her intrigue, and hopped into his souped-up yellow Twingo one hot June afternoon after college. Off they whizzed together down leafy country lanes to his home village, just north of Shrewsbury, where the church with its squat little tower overlooked a babbling stream and the pretty green.

"How lovely!" said Sally, admiring the medieval wood carvings and beautiful stained glass that cast a kaleidoscope of coloured flecks across the pews and nave. She followed him with increasing excitement up to the tiny swirly-carpeted ringing room. There, he unhooked the tie from the wall and lowered the ropes down to proudly show her his spider. To be honest, it looked rather ugly to Sally's mind, but she remembered that he had crafted it by hand for his A-level DT coursework, so did her best to sound impressed.

"Do you want to see the bells themselves?" he asked her. "They're up there." He pointed at the rickety-looking ladder in the corner.

"Of course!" exclaimed Sally, who had a good head for heights. And so up they went, so she could take a proper look at his light three.

"Funny," said Sally, as she ran her hand across the cool, hard crown of the two-hundredweight tenor. "From the way you described it, I imagined it would be bigger than this."

"It's what you do with it that counts," replied Little Rob, blushing. "Although, admittedly, there's not that much you can do with a three. Before you know it, you've run out of options. But I've already spoken to the vicar and I'm washing cars every Saturday to raise funds for an augmentation."

"What's that?" asked Sally.

"It's where you add more bells so you end up with a bigger set," explained Rob. "I've had it all measured up and, although it will be a bit of a complicated operation with a fair bit of chopping and changing, it should certainly be possible. You see, for most people, it's more effort than it's worth to come out on a Wednesday night for just a little three like this, but if I can get a bigger set, I should be able to get a proper band to come and do some interesting stuff with it. There's loads you can do with a half decent six."

"Sounds ideal," said Sally.

Back in the present from her little reminiscence, Sally pinged Little Rob a quick reply: *"I'm a Surprise Major ringer now, believe it or not. Still finding Bristol a handful, though, if I'm honest. How did you get on with your augmentation?"*

A long pause before the reply eventually came.

"Didn't go through with that in the end. Just had to accept that it was a bit unrealistic on the finance front."

"That's a shame," replied Sally. *"But it's good to make*

the most of what you've got. I'm more of a heavy eight girl myself these days, but I'm sure there must be plenty of beginners out there who'd like to have a go on a quirky little three."

"Maybe..."

Then everything went strangely quiet.

Was it something I said? Sally wondered, and decided to message him a timid *"Have I upset you?"* plus sad-face emoji, and then, when no reply came, a solitary sad little question mark. But that was that. Within a week, his Ringr profile had disappeared and Sally never heard another peep out of Little Rob Boyle again.

Oh well, she consoled herself, maybe it just wasn't to be, and, although she hadn't seen him in the flesh, she was pretty sure the intervening years were unlikely to have changed anything for the better where his height was concerned. A future with Little Rob Boyle would have to have been lived exclusively in very flat shoes, even outside of the ringing room, so on balance it was no great loss. Besides, he would only ever have been a pale substitute for his magnificent namesake. Perhaps spinsterdom was what Sally was destined for, and what she should just resign herself to. At least she still had her rodents for company....

And then a sudden vision of Robert came to her. The other Robert. The Robert that she really wanted. Rugby Bob, as she most fondly thought of him - oh, those rock-solid legs from God's own workshop! And she could imagine him miraculously returned to her one sunny Sunday afternoon, shirtless in the heat, on his hands and knees, surrounded by twigs and straw, helping her to muck out her beaver. *Oh, come back to me! Bob, Bob, dear sweet Bob...!*

And just as this yearning was possessing her, gripping every fibre of her being, Sally heard the unmistakable sound of something coming through the letterbox, the flap snapping back elastically. Christine the capybara, who had been trained like a dog to fetch, trotted in with an airmail letter clenched in her ample muzzle. Sally recognised the handwriting instantly: *Bob!*

Perhaps he hasn't forgotten about me! she thought to herself with mounting excitement as she tore the envelope open and whipped out the fragile sheet of paper inside. *Maybe he does love me more than the CCCCCCR after all!*

And she started to read…

"My darling Sally - or do you still want me to call you Observation? - No, I think Sally is better. You don't really need me to call you Observation any more, do you? Not after all that we have been through together.

Sally,

Oh, how I have missed you these past weeks! Every time I think of our enforced separation, it stabs right through me like the unbearable agony of a late backstroke lead. Each moment without you is like waiting to be released from an endless series of bobs at the back of Stedman, and not knowing whether to go in quick or slow. Oh, the torture of uncertainty! Every time I try to visualise your beautiful face, my memory deceives me and I hate myself for the things that I forget, like the blue line for Belfast. How can you love something so much, and yet still the finer details, that were once so clear and obvious, have suddenly slipped away, become so fluid and nebulous? Sometimes, in my memory, your eyes have a grass-green tint. Other times, they are as blue as the Indian Ocean. And sometimes, even, they are silver, glittering with violet flashes. Oh, what colour are your eyes, now, this very moment? If only I could stare deep into them, I promise that I would never forget!

But I am being an incorrigible romantic, aren't I, dearest Sally? And I must save some space on this sorry sheet of paper to tell you why I have been so silent. You must hate me for my neglect, I am sure, but please, I beg of you, read on and all will be explained..."

A tear was already forming in Sally's eye, born of a 23-spliced conundrum of mixed emotions: joy, relief, doubt, anger, fear... What was he about to tell her?

She barely had the power or the courage to read on, but she had to, oh how she had to!

"Firstly, a confession. Lundy was nothing but an elaborate hoax! Forgive me, Sally, for not telling you sooner, but I had good reason…"

Sally was agog. So the CCCCCCR was not in fact running its own Guantanamo Bay for the correction of criminal ringers? *Thick-Skinned Bell Ringers* were not being hunted down and sentenced to the Bristol Channel gulag? It wasn't a punishable offence to ring Pudsey, or even Rutland, after all? It had all seemed so probable at the time, and yet, now that she thought about it, perhaps it was all a bit far-fetched. The CCCCCCR wasn't tyrannical, as such. It was just, well, dogmatic. It had gone a bit authoritarian with all of the COVID ringing strictures, for example, but it was all for the greater good, and nobody could deny that.

"Lundy was merely a diversion tactic, so that the wider ringing community would not cotton on to the higher purpose to which I, and a mere handful of the Reservist Ringers, have been selected. Do you want to know what this higher purpose is, my darling?"

Yes! thought Sally. *Yes, I do! For God's sake, get on with it!*

"As you will be aware, the year in which we find ourselves

is 2022. You will understand what a significant milestone this is for our dear Sovereign..."

Of course! exclaimed Sally to herself. *Seventy years on the throne!*

"And so, in celebration of this truly auspicious occasion, Sir Richard Branson's state-of-the-art Virgin Foundry has cast the Platinum Jubilee Bells, of which I am to be one of the ringers!"

Oh, how wonderful! gasped Sally. She read on, clutching the sheet in eager anticipation of further details...

"What's more, now that the putting-them-on-a-boat thing has been done, Sir Richard has gone one better! The bells are, as we speak, being installed in a specially commissioned Airbus A380, which will carry Her Majesty the Queen to all thirty destinations on her Jubilee tour. A rotating golden throne will be placed in the centre of the circle and, so that we humble representatives of the ringing fraternity might bestow our gratitude upon her for her seventy years of service, the Queen will sit and listen to non-stop mile-high peals and long lengths rung mid-flight (apart from on the Heathrow-Amsterdam leg, when it will just have to be a quick quarter of something Minimus).

Her Majesty knows nothing of this little surprise, which was thought up by the Prince of Wales, and I am sworn to secrecy. I tell you, dearest Sally, only because I know I can trust you not to gossip about it on Facebook Bellringers or, heaven forbid, Thick-Skinned! Needless to say, the long and arduous flights that the Queen would have been expecting to endure in tedious silence will instead bring her measureless joy, surrounded as she will be for hours on end by the unmistakable English music of bells in full voice! I dare say she will be so enraptured that it will be a job to disembark her by the time we get to Kuala Lumpur or Perth!

By way of preparation for this unique test of our endurance, we happy few, we band of ringers have actually all been taken to Lundy for some serious high-level advance training run by crack ART teachers. They're really putting us through our paces, let me tell you! They certainly take no prisoners. Fluff a Pink's Single and it's three laps of the island with no supper!"

Sally was gripped by the thrill of imagining how stimulating all of this must be, when quite out of the blue, her joy was shattered by this hideous revelation...

"The fortunate ringers who have been selected for this honour are myself (of course!), Ed Stocks, Kat Sears, Lee Drong, Tess Stringer..."

TESS STRINGER? Sally's heart skipped a beat, maybe even two... *What was she doing there?!* Tess was famous throughout the tintinnalogical universe, and was known for hanging around new bell projects like a bad smell, batting her ridiculous false eyelashes to make sure that she could muscle in on anything new and exciting. She spent every free moment that she had volunteering on an unpaid basis at Meltham, Downe and Bymore. She stuck her oar in to give advice while they were making the moulds, got involved while they were firing up the furnace, and after they'd poured it, she was always on hand to give her opinion on how best to flick off the slag.

And so it was that she wheedled her way into getting herself trained up through the back door and, having flirted her way through the apprenticeship in record time, she ultimately broke the glass ceiling to become that absurdly rare bird: a fully-fledged female bell hanger. *The One Show* reported on her achievement with great fanfare. The way she fawned over Matt Baker whilst demonstrating how to deal with a stiff clapper that wouldn't swing freely - truly nauseating! The nickname she gained from that little escapade - The Clapper Slapper - summed it up perfectly. It was, of course, extremely unkind of people to be cynical about Tess breaking through in a male-dominated profession, but it was hard to hail the success of a woman whose well-publicised antics were of the variety that would make Stormy Daniels blush.

The worst thing about Tess Stringer, though, was just

how bloody good she was at ringing. It was jealousy on Sally's part, pure and simple, and deep down she knew it. All those months it had taken her to master Bristol, and still it wasn't perfect, even now. Tess, on the other hand, was faultless on the Bristol front, every time. Her points were so sharp you could have used them to pierce a climate protester's septum, and her back work was no less impeccable than the front. Sally could just imagine her, way up there, thirty-thousand feet above the Maldives, simpering away in that thick Black Country accent of hers, with all of her usual false modesty - *"Oh, I don't know if I can remember what happens at the Glasgow half-lead. Will you tell me what to do if I come unstuck?"* - and all of those drooling fools like Martin Draycott would be taken in by it.

But what would Robert do if Tess tried to tempt him with experimental touches, touches that grew slowly and inexorably to Exploding Tittums at the pivotal lead head? Could he say no to the Delights of Dudley's own Delilah? He was just a man, after all… *Oh God, what if he can't resist introducing her to his Velvet Willy, and she gets her first blows on it before me?* Tess Stringer, with those Kylie hotpants, three inches of unbleached roots and her impossibly slick nails. She was there, and Sally wasn't! What was she going to do with her Bob?!

The thought was unbearable, and Sally just had to put it to the back of her mind. She read the rest of the letter as quickly as she could, so as not to worsen the agony of the clappers that pounded on the soundbow of her heart.

"As soon as we have completed the world tour, I will return to you, Sally, my darling, and we will get to work on those new bells. Please just wait for me a little longer. A few more weeks, then the whole future will be ours!"

Sally let the tear-stained sheet slip from her fingers and spiral to the floor like a wounded butterfly. How would she get through the loneliness of the endless days and nights ahead, stuck here on her own at Girthsmount Hill, all the time terrified that Robert might be swayed by the allure of the dreaded Tess? And when he did eventually return after the glamour of all those jet-set peals, would he be quite literally brought back down to earth by the disappointing reality of Sally's lacklustre touches? How could she possibly ever hope to measure up?

There was no other option. She had to go into some serious training. She would have to put Mike's Electrobonger® into her Hewlett-Packard and get all of the must-do methods under her belt. The Standard Eight was pretty much sorted already, of course, but she still needed to work on certain aspects of the Pickled Egg. There was also the rough outline of Mike's Battered Sausage to chew on and if she pushed him to get the project moving forward during the August recess, then she would be up to speed before Robert returned and - more importantly - before Tess Stringer knew anything about it! A quick glance at BellBoard confirmed that Tess had no prior experience of Brown Willy, and her history in terms of Cocking Alliance only ran to a single outing: a quarter, and that had been back in 2013.

Sally could see the masterplan forming in her mind. If she could get enough of the competent locals together for regular practice and some intensive group pricking workshops, at which she could show them the ins and outs of her Fanybong, Robert's Velvet Willy, and their beautiful Frotting Alliance, then when Robert returned, he would find himself in amongst some of the best peal ringers in the country. As for Tess, well, she could clear off and find some other band of poodle-fakers to fawn over her Bristol Max.

And so, Sally got to work, emailing the usual suspects, attaching downloads from Blue Line and suggesting suitable practice towers. (Sloley Fealingham was an obvious option: the bells there were decent enough and available any time you wanted them, even if the tower itself was in a fairly sorry state of neglect. Not to worry, though: they could use the opportunity to build up their collective stamina *Karate Kid*-style by doing some voluntary clearing out of the pigeon shit, jackdaws' nests and empty cans of Castrol GTX.) Crispin was good enough for Surprise Major now, and Hurricane

Hazel, well, it had been quite a while since she had wreaked havoc on Cornwall, but she had managed to do some substantial rebuilding work since then, so she should at least be able to hold things together in plain courses. Bev Belleau, Dominic Topp, Fleet Carr, plus Derek and Mike to make up the eight. *It could be a strong band with enough practice,* thought Sally. *And who knows, by the time Robert comes back to me, I might be ready for my first long length!*

Sally's reverie was shattered by the sudden sound of footsteps coming up the spiral stairs. As was often the way, several of the regulars would wait outside in the car park until they knew Derek had finished with Muriel, not wanting to form an awkward audience to the messy spectacle. They would then congregate at the foot of the steps and enter *en masse*, heaving themselves up by the rope that was screwed to the wall in lieu of a bannister rail, puffing and wheezing as they went, for the most part.

First through the door was Hazel Fluck, who had scraped her hair up into an unexpectedly tight bun and located the most feminine of her ringing jumpers (Dennis the Menace angora) in preference to the customary unhygienic dungarees. Sensible turquoise leggings and double-knotted Doc Martens completed the look: nobody could deny that this was a woman who had arrived in the ringing room with the express intention to practise safe ringing.

It was particularly important this week that safe ringing was observed, as Hazel and Derek had been given prior warning of a visit from Bertha Gorse. Bertha was the Midlands-region chair of the

CCCCCCR's own affiliated inspectorate, Bell-Ringing Education, Accountability and Standards (BREASts), the new touchy-feely rebranding for the dreaded institution formerly known as OfStaB (The Office for Standards in Bell-Ringing). Bertha was an indomitable force in the world of BREASts, her reputation undeniably going before her.

"We'll all need to be on our best behaviour!" Hazel had emailed to everyone, putting the exclamation mark to indicate light-heartedness and to disguise obvious panic. Sally had wondered why the *'The Bells May Be Up! Do Not Touch!'* sign had made a triumphant return in pride of place next to the Quality Street, even though the bells hadn't actually been left up since the last Frotting wedding, which was so far back in the distant past that the ensuing marriage had in the meantime resulted in three blond children, two black Labradors, a Shetland pony, several upgrades of the happy couple's his-n-hers hire purchase VW Tiguans and, more recently, to the joy of the coffee morning gossiping collective, a poorly concealed affair with the Ukrainian nanny...

Bursting past Hazel in his usual explosion of bouncy barking came Hastings, her shaggy Labradoodle.

"Hastings! Stay!" bellowed Hazel. Hastings duly ignored her, as was his wont, and bounded over to Sally for his usual dose of pre-ringing fuss. He knew he would eventually have to curl up over by the books and endure ninety minutes of maddening frustration, watching these people yanking fluffy toys up and down, which they would never once throw in his direction to catch and savage in wild, slobbery joy. So, he reasoned in his canine simplicity, he had better make the most of things while he could and give Sally a jolly good licking. Sally was the most saltily lickable of all the humans that Hastings met up with on a Tuesday night. Veronica tasted of lavender soap, Crispin tasted of Paco Rabanne, and Derek Beavis tasted like the hairy things that Hastings periodically rediscovered in the corners of his basket. He didn't know what any of the others tasted like, as they were all pretty standoffish where lick greetings were concerned and would turn away or push him back before he got the chance.

"Hastings! That's enough now," commanded Hazel in her best Barbara Woodhouse voice and Hastings knew that his few seconds of gay abandon were very much over. He slunk over to the bookshelf and curled up, whimpering, in readiness for the long evening ahead. "Sorry about that," she continued to Sally. "You know how he is…"

"It's fine," said Sally with a reassuring smile. "I know he's only trying to be friendly." She mused ruefully on the realisation that the dog's was the only foreign saliva with which she had come into regular contact since Bob went AWOL. What's more, she realised,

Hastings' attraction probably had not so much to do with her *per se*, as it did with the smell of her beaver.

Hazel went over to Hastings, squatted down and squirted out a pouch onto a commemorative Charles & Diana wedding saucer, which would keep him occupied for a few moments. It was Tesco's own-brand rabbit and turkey in gravy, which was one of his favourites, so it certainly did the trick.

"Has anybody seen the ringing register?" asked Hazel, rifling through the books behind Hastings, and those piled up on the floor, that couldn't be housed in the limited shelf space.

"Ringing register?" asked Derek. "Do we even have one?"

"Of course we do, Derek," insisted Hazel pointedly, in case Bertha Gorse was within earshot. "We do everything by the book here, don't we, wink wink? Aha! Got it!" Reaching past Hastings' heavily wagging tail, she fished out the dusty clipboard that had been lying horizontally on the bottom shelf. In the process, she managed to flip Hastings' saucer over unawares and shower gravy all over one of Derek's treasured ringing volumes. Fortunately, Derek didn't notice either, and Hastings promptly dealt with the problem, contenting himself with licking Dove until it was cleaner than it had been in years. It was Hastings' little contribution towards

Hazel's nascent plan to "sort out this pigsty of a tower once and for all".

Two weeks previously, Hazel had been up to her eyeballs with tower captain admin. What with the district tower open day less than a month away, she had been getting nervous about the impression that the current ringing room might give. All of the tower notices had been handwritten decades ago by Mr Beavis' wife at her weekly calligraphy class in Much Wenlock and were now sadly faded, dog-eared and graffitied:

Strictly No ~~Talking~~ RINGING
Whilst Others Are ~~Ringing~~ TALKING

This, for example, had appeared in red marker pen after a visiting band of Liverpool students had come to try out Frotting and nobody had ever bothered to rectify it, given that it pretty much summed up the actual ethos of the place.

No, it would all have to be replaced and, thanks to her trusty Facit TP2 typewriter, Hazel would be the one to drag Frotting into the mid-twentieth century, at least where strategy and marketing were concerned. And so, she had made it her mission systematically to work through the transcription of all of the tower's documentation. The previous week, it had been the turn of the information regarding the clock to be given the Hazel treatment. The original text was to be found in a pale green Silvine exercise book, rendered in unnecessarily florid calligraphy by Mrs Beavis and dated 1979. Fortunately, the information itself was accurate, given that no significant works had been carried out on the clock since the time of free school milk.

'St James the Dismembered has perhaps the most magnificent clock in all of South Shropshire and the Marches...' read Hazel to herself as she tapped away on her rickety Facit. She was a touch-typist of nigh-on thirty years' standing, so did not need to glance once at the keys or the creamy Basildon Bond onto which the words appeared like footprints in the snow. 'Of all the clocks in the area, St James' has the best reputation both for quality and timing...' It all sounded a bit on the grandiose side to Hazel, who preferred to stick to facts rather than venturing into the minefield of opinions. However, there would be all hell to pay with the committee if she re-worded any of the time-honoured tower liturgies, so she resolved to copy away without a further moment's hesitation, drifting in and out of focus on the words themselves, as with a bedtime Martina Cole that you just can't seem to get into: '...problems caused by the excessive weight of the original clock hammers caused considerable damage which had to be urgently addressed… *blah blah blah...* huge exposed clock mechanism which was vulnerable both to the elements and rodent infestations… *blah blah blah…* a very unusual clock face which is thought to have originated in medieval Flanders… *blah blah blah…* much debate about how to restore the old clock, particularly regarding the best way to clean it and its inner workings…'

Finally, Hazel took a moment to stretch out her fingers and glanced up at her handiwork. *Damn and blast it!* she thought. She had quite forgotten that her L key had finally given up the ghost whilst typing out the 37th copy of last year's Advent pew sheet. But the irritation was short-lived. *Oh well,* she reasoned. *Nobody is going to notice. And even if they do, the context should make it all perfectly clear what the information pertains to.* And with that, she scrolled down for a final paragraph and engaged the caps lock - 'IF YOU WISH TO VIEW THE COCK, JUST ASK THE TOWER CAPTAIN, WHO CAN TAKE YOU UP THE TOWER AND GIVE YOU A GUIDED TOUR.'

Thinking it wise not to attempt to sign off as 'Hazel Fluck', she decided instead to bypass the 'L' quandary altogether and go with 'The Committee', which, whilst blander, would at least be future-proofed in the event of her own untimely demise.

And, little did she realise, but an untimely demise could well be on the cards for Hurricane Hazel, whose latest wave of devastation had been wrought upon Belfast, much to the fury of her fellow peal ringers. She had crashed her way through it, mercilessly uprooting the line and letting it fly off into the middle of the Irish Sea like the tail of a rogue, shredded kite. Scarcely a single place had been left undamaged and every point was mercilessly wrenched free of its moorings and flattened beyond recognition. Three attempts had been made, none of which went beyond twenty-five minutes, and, thanks to Hazel, all that they had managed to produce with their Belfast was a sound akin to a series of car bombs detonating in the Falls Road, circa 1974.

However, for now at least, Hazel was blissfully unaware that the ringing community was poised to take action against her ongoing atrocities. (People in a certain WhatsApp group for local ringers had even mooted kidnapping her and dumping her, hog-tied in a jute sack, in Reception at the start of the next Bradfield Ringing Course, so that they could sort out her sodding place bells for her.) But no, Hazel's ringing ability was the least of her worries. Her top priority in this precise moment, with Bertha Gorse advancing like a cloud of poison gas, was the little matter of Compliance…

"Right," commanded Hazel with schoolmarmish firmness, "let's get this attendance sheet filled in! Derek?"

"Present."

"Muriel?"

"Here."

And so it went on, as the rest of the battalion trooped in in single file through the door in varying states of dampness as per the wisdom of their choice of rainwear. By the time everyone present had signed in, Hazel could see that, quite extraordinarily, they had a full cohort. In addition to Derek, Muriel, Sally, Mike and herself, Veronica had managed to drag herself away from the semi-finals of *I'm a Spliced Surprise Maximus Ringer... Get Me Out of Here!* The nation had been gripped for weeks by the contestants' unending nightmare, abandoned as they were to fend for themselves in the middle of the Lincolnshire fens with access to only a mismatched, tinny four, whose plain bearings hadn't been greased in decades. Oh, how they suffered, having to ring bumpy Minimus or Singles with a cover, week in week out, and then forced to choke down soggy fig rolls and weak tea with dried skimmed milk for the gruesome entertainment of the viewers back home! Naturally, it was the highlight of Veronica's televisual year.

"She must be really serious about this Reverse Canterbury quarter to miss *I'm an SSMR*," whispered Sally to Mike, naughtily. That said, it was more likely that Veronica had got her husband Jim down on all fours to fiddle with her digibox, so that she could watch it later on catch-up instead.

Phyllis had come along too, of course. Phyllis was one of those *"I only do Grandsire"* people, who clearly had a deep-seated and all-consuming envy of anyone else's attempts to try something different. For her, seeing Veronica's Reverse Canterbury laid open for public ridicule on a weekly basis had become a source of deep, secret joy. Encouraging words like *"Ooh, you nearly had it there"* and *"Better luck next time. That was a really good try!"* did little to disguise the obvious thrill she derived from her friend's repeated failure, and you could be sure that now Veronica had her quarter peal attempt pencilled into Derek's little diary, Phyllis would be taking her weekly front-row seat at practice night with Quality Street at the ready, in lieu of popcorn.

"I can't remember the last time I saw weather as bad

as this," said Veronica, as she hung up her sopping mac. "Puts you in mind of the Lynmouth flood of '52. I doubt the septic tanks over at the campsite are going to cope. All those caravans with their dreadful little masturbating toilets. There'll be some clearing up for the owners to do tomorrow!" Veronica was in her element when it came to identifying and passing comment on mess, whether it be made by man, beast or The Good Lord himself. She was even more in her element when identifying whose responsibility it was to deal with it. Needless to say, it was never her own.

"Anybody want to take these courgettes off my hands?" interrupted Phyllis. "They're on the cusp of entering the marrow stage, but I think I've picked them just in time." She wielded two of the handsome specimens fished out from inside her Waitrose bag.

"Don't talk to me about fruit and veg," said Veronica, holding up a firm hand by way of refusal. "We're up to our eyeballs around this time of the year. I've been trying to offload Jim's plums for the past fortnight, but to no avail. I'm just going to have to do a whole weekend of jamming, that's all there is to it!"

Next through the door came Dominic Topp, gasping for relief at having come through the storm intact. He was freshly arrived back from his week of trying out some of mid-Wales' finest organs. "What a week!"

he announced to everyone as he plonked himself down wetly next to Sally, who passed him a handy guest towel that she had spare in her bag. "I don't think I could have fitted in another organ if I'd tried!" And whilst rubbing himself off, he handed her his i-Phone so she could view the snaps he'd taken of the fabulous, milky-white stop knobs of Cwmshott.

Dominic was obsessed with organs of all shapes and sizes, and thought nothing of travelling the length and breadth of the country if it meant that he could have a bit of a play. Indeed, he was blitzing his way through the National Pipe Organ Register at an ever-increasing rate, and whilst he accepted that ticking off all 35,000+ entries might be a tall order, he would certainly soon be up there as one of the most experienced organ grabbers of all time.

"How are you getting on at Granser?" Sally asked him. "I imagine it's quite nice having such a big one all to yourself."

"Oh yes," he said. "It's an honour to be let loose on such a magnificent instrument. Nice to be able to showcase my skills and get the word around a bit, too. I've just had the Frotting vicar on the phone, as a matter of fact, asking if I'll come and fill in with running the choir now that your Mrs Cattiton has said she refuses to do any more Christmas services. I hear that last year was the straw that broke the camel's back…"

"Oh God!" said Sally, grimacing at the memory. "The way those toddlers were allowed to stampede unsupervised around the crib and tear the plastic baby Jesus limb from limb during 'What Child Is This?' - I've never seen anything like it! Mrs Cattiton was a nervous wreck by the time it got round to 'O Come All Ye Faithful'. Visibly trembling, and I swear her hair had turned a shade whiter by the end. I hope that you'll not have quite such a hard time yourself this year. Word to the wise: pull out all the stops and just try to drown it out when the screaming starts."

"Noted," said Dom, who was already beginning to wonder if he might have bitten off more than he could chew. (Now that he came to think of it, there'd been talk a while back of how Ruth Gillon-Smith wouldn't touch the Frotting gig with a barge pole. The vicar went down on bended knee, by all accounts, to get her to nip over straight after playing for Clungefunton, explaining that Mrs Cattiton was laid up in bed with another flare-up of her oilseed rape allergy. Ruth, however, was firm in her refusal to take on the unenviable challenge of Frotting for a family service, Clungefunton already being more than enough of a handful, thank you very much.) *Oh well,* thought Dom, *what the hell? As long as there's free mulled wine on tap and that Muriel doesn't come anywhere near me with her Wensleydale Unmentionables, it can't be all that bad, can it…?*

Coming in soon after Dom was Bev, who had also been away for the week, but the manner of her arrival was the opposite of Dominic's. She looked decidedly down-hearted and, with thinly-veiled pleasure, Muriel could sense immediately that Bev had had something of a comeuppance.

"Bev!" cried Derek. "How lovely to see you again!" Bev was always a bit suspicious of how lovely Derek found it to see her, but his interest was harmless enough, she supposed. "And how radiant you're looking!"

"Yes," added Veronica. "I was just thinking, *There's a woman who's been off to pamper herself at Granser Facials.* Am I right?"

"Well, just a quick quarter peel this time," said Bev, blushing at the attention her freshly stripped complexion was garnering from all and sundry. "I only go in for the full peel once in a blue moon these days. It really takes it out of me, and I get through gallons of Nivea Q10 calming it all down again afterwards. Besides," she added, batting the last few raindrops off her bright pink Aquascutum, "I was a bit worn out after Portsmouth..."

"Of course!" cried Mike. "The Spliced Girls on tour! How did it go?" (He knew how Bev's little outing to Portsmouth Cathedral had gone, of course, because

BellBoard and Facebook had already revealed all, but better to feign ignorance and act normal.)

"Knocked out in the quarter finals," admitted Bev despondently. "I was livid! That awful Leah Beece woman from the Essex Association took marks off for all manner of silly, pedantic things! She said our points weren't sharp enough and she was positively rude about Mrs McRocker's Double Dublin, even though everyone knew she was in constant physical pain!"

"Ada? In pain?" asked Phyllis, who knew Mrs McRocker from the local Scottish country dancing scene. "Was it the ankle again?"

"Yes," confirmed Bev. "I advised her not to go to that reduced mobility ceilidh up at the Willey estate the other week, what with her sore bunions on top of everything else, but she won't be told. She tripped over the wheelchair and turned her ankle while she was Stripping the Willow with Lady Boyes. So now it's the Ralgex and Tubigrip routine all over again. There'll be no more Gay Gordons for her for a good long while, put it that way..."

Bev failed to mention that the extreme low point of Portsmouth was nothing to do with Ada, but rather, it was Bev's own doing, namely the way in which she had misstruck Yorkshire at the triple 5-6 down dodge pretty much every time. In fact, it earned her the unenviable new nickname amongst her fellow Spliced Girls of 'The Yorkshire Clipper'. Her silence on this was, of course, fruitless, as it had been all over *Thick-Skinned Bell Ringers* within moments of its occurrence, along with all manner of inappropriate emojis.

'The Spliced Girls', incidentally, was how the Ladies' Guild Surprise Major group jovially referred to themselves, and they convened every Friday morning at the quaint little tower of Overmill, just south of Bridgnorth. They chose Overmill both for its lovely, easy-going bells and for its hideous filth and disorganisation, which made Sloley Fealingham look like an operating theatre. This choice of tower allowed them to put their prowess as volunteer-minded ladies to good use with Mr Sheen and bin bags.

When they had first turned up, fifty years of squirrel-chewed sallies, mouldy *Ringing Worlds* and Quality Street wrappers lay in drifts across a threadbare, orange carpet that had last consorted with a Hoover in 1963. As a tower whose regular ringers had comprised only train-obsessed heterosexual widowers for as long as anyone could remember, it was little surprise that nobody had paid much attention to hygiene or general cleanliness at Overmill. With the tower captain, Jack Brace, now in his nineties and barely able to get up the stairs, Bev had taken on the job in hand and done a deal, whereby in exchange for an hour and a half of ringing, they would spend another half-hour decluttering and sanitizing for as many weeks as it took to get things ship-shape again. Little did she realise how long the work would take, and over time, the Spliced Girls had come to regard the cleaning as a Sisyphean task, not unlike the task of mastering ringing, in fact. They just put on their Marigolds - both for the ringing and the cleaning - and got on with it.

The Spliced Girls used their Fridays at Overmill to prepare studiously for the Ladies' Guild Knock-Out competition and they were - or at least Bev was - convinced that it would be a walk in the park. After all, how many other ladies-only bands were there who could possibly splice Painswick, Double Dublin, Deva and Yorkshire as well as them, if at all? Little did anyone realise that a ringing resistance movement to English domination had been secretly forming on the other side of the Channel... A small group of militant feminists based in Toulouse, seeking a bit of down time from smashing the local phallocentric patriarchy, had caught wind of the new ring of ten in the Pyrenees and decided that it was high time that an activity overrun with English men should be shaken up a bit by French women. And so, within the space of twelve months, through hard work and unwavering dedication to the cause, The Vernet Lesbians, as they called themselves, had mastered the Standard Eight and moved on to some of the 'more interesting' methods that everybody kept arguing about on Facebook. They were, however, not going to be told by 'some man or other' what was hot and what was not. Just because everyone in the rest of the ringing fraternity - *misogynistic concept, if ever there was one!* - was currently obsessing like sex-crazed teenage boys over the likes of Turramurra and Cooktown Orchid, that would not stop the Vernet Lesbians from ploughing their own furrow. Stolidly refusing to follow the latest fads, they resolved to be ground-breaking and experimental, trying out long touches of Clitheroe, for example, in a female-only space that was safe from the intrusions of ringing's perennial mansplainers.

And so, when the Ladies Guild of Change Ringers had chosen Portsmouth as the venue for their first International Women's Knock-Out Competition, the Lesbians forged the single-minded plan to hop on the ferry from Le Havre, compete for the trophy in the name of St Joan, and bring it back in triumph to Vernet. After a hard day's ringing, it looked as if their plan was coming to fruition, and there they were, in the final! With Bev's Spliced Girls already knocked out and the other fancied band from the Chester Guild firing out in the semis, all that stood in the way of the Vernet Lesbians were three vehicle paintwork repairwomen and five members of the Guild of Change-Ringing Eczema Sufferers, who had formed a last-minute scratch band, and, against all the odds, made it all the way to the grand final. Bev listened in with barely concealed fury as both bands turned in near-faultless performances. It should have been her up there, calling her immaculately crafted composition, not these French upstarts and cobbled-together also-rans who had just got lucky! In the end, it was to Vernet that the judge awarded the trophy, commenting that their leads were just that little bit crisper, and also that they deserved extra credit for originality in their unorthodox inclusion of Gropenhole.

"Oh well," said Muriel, when Bev had finished recounting her tale of woe. "Better luck next time." She unwrapped an Orange Creme and let it sit on her tongue, savouring the sweet taste of schadenfreude.

Hazel, who had been listening in on the whole story whilst continuing with her register, felt a tinge of envy that she had missed the event, given that she was usually one of the Spliced Girls' stalwarts. It was quite something for Bev to steal some of Hazel's usual thunder where responsibility for ringing disasters of legendary magnitude was concerned, as The Hurricane had pretty much cornered the local market in recent years. To be able to share the mantle of fallibility with someone else for a while was something of a relief for Hazel, who knew all too well how far her reputation went before her. Perhaps she would be able to put tentative feelers out to be involved in the next Spliced Girls quarter if Bev, as predicted, would need time to go off and lick her wounds...

The Women's Knock-Out had sadly not been a possibility for Hazel this year. It clashed with Hastings' annual worming day, which involved several hours of tricking him into eating the tablet, waiting for him to throw it back up and then repeating the process with a fresh ball of Pedigree Chum. (Hazel liked to stick to routines where the dog was concerned: if the calendar said the 27th of August, then the 27th of August it was to be.) Besides, she would get to meet the Vernet Lesbians another way before too long, she was sure. As soon as Hastings got his pet passport through, she could plan a little road trip to the Pyrenees and meet them on home turf. She could even set up a little workshop to show them how to grease their nipples and check their flanges for cracks, experienced bell-maintenance experts being probably quite thin on the ground down there near the Spanish border.

Yes, that is what she would do, decided Hazel, and she made a mental note to see if the camper van would be likely to cope with the journey. Besides, it was the perfect excuse to stop putting it off and get underneath for a spot of welding to her undercarriage, plus she could scrub down her claggy mud flaps while she was at it before winter took hold. *A stitch in time,* she said to herself... *A stitch in time...*

Interrupting Hazel's little daydream with his sudden arrival, was Crispin Hipkiss. "Evening, everyone," said Crispin, with a slight tremor of apprehension in his voice. "I hope you don't mind, but they've found a crack in one of the flanges at Clungefunton, so I've brought my mother along again with me." Crispin could detect from the involuntary expressions of horror on the faces all around him that this was not a welcome piece of news, as Hazel frantically scribbled something on the clipboard and lunged for the visitors' book.

"Bloody hell!" announced Mrs Hipkiss as she manoeuvred herself pelvically up the final step and into the ringing chamber. "I've had more hot flushes today than a Japanese toilet! Crispin! Get me a chair!"

"In a minute, mother."

"I'm telling you now, Crispin," she shrilled, "I carried you for nine months, remember, and now my body's paying for it." (No, he didn't remember, thankfully, but she wasn't one to be contradicted, so he let it go.) "I'm never going back to that bloody gynaecologist again. My undercarriage feels like a sausage skin trying to hold back a gallon of custard. Pass me the bag with my pads in it, would you, just in case?"

Even though Dympna Hipkiss had only been to Frotting three or four times, everybody already knew her intimately. She didn't give them much choice, if the truth be told. Her conversation - or rather, her monologue - rarely veered away from matters medical, and for the most part, that entailed graphic blow-by-blow accounts of her experience of the menopause and its specific side-effects. It was as if she had been told by the gynaecologist to keep a diary and, instead of writing it down, she just spoke the thoughts out loud, wherever and whenever they came to her. Everyone at Frotting, therefore, whether they liked it or not, already had a full and graphic understanding of Dympna's internal falseness.

Dympna was very new to ringing, having decided to take it up so as to keep a closer eye on Crispin. She was pathologically suspicious of anything that her son appeared to enjoy, assuming that that meant he was being 'led astray' in some way. That was the Catholic in her: Crispin having fun might mean that romance was on the cards, romance with a very probably unsuitable woman. Dympna had already singled out 'that Sally' as a cause for concern, with her long dark hair and innocent-looking eyes. Sally almost certainly had designs on her Crispin, Dympna decided, or she would have, if she wasn't clever enough to realise that his mother had her eye on her... Dympna gave Sally a weak smile of recognition as she took her seat and helped herself to a Noisette Triangle. "Sit here next to me, Crispin," she commanded, "and fan me with that magazine. I'm burning up here!"

Crispin flapped the *Ringing World* lazily at his mother's cherry-red cheeks whilst she rummaged in her handbag to find her Plain Hunt and a capsule of Evening Primrose oil.

"You can probably use a courgette, can't you, Crispin?" asked Phyllis, waving one in front of his nose. "Makes a lovely gratin!"

"Oh yes," agreed Dympna, "he likes a nice bit of veg, does my Crispin. Seems to be constantly sending his friends little pictures of aubergines on his phone. I think they must all be in some sort of a growing club." Crispin's toes curled invisibly inside his shoes, but he didn't say anything. "Just look at him, though - nothing but skin and bone! I know everyone's into this healthy eating thing these days, but I think he'd be much better off if he got a decent bit of meat inside him once in a while..."

Whilst his mother's verbal diarrhoea continued on into overdrive, Crispin seized the moment to completely block it out and to gaze over surreptitiously through the corner of his eye at Dom...

Lovely Dom! Crispin hadn't felt this way since Robert had turned up out of the blue, with his shaggy brown locks, piercing blue eyes and rugby-player thighs so rock-solid that you could use them to loosen castellated nuts with. But sadly, he had soon realised that he was climbing up the wrong tower ladder where Robert was concerned: Robert was as straight as a Stedman tenor line. Dominic Topp, on the other hand, was a different kettle of fish altogether. All the signs were there when they had both ended up going on the same ringing weekend to Cumbria. Crispin had been far too shy to make the first move, but Dom's standing behind him in his spray-on jeans to talk him through his first blows on the tenor at Cockermouth, well, that had really broken the ice. The more they got to know each other over the rest of the weekend, the more Crispin felt that, in the right circumstances and with a bit of cajoling, Dom might very well be persuaded to go up wrong.

Dom was on Ringr, Crispin had noted within seconds of meeting him. Then again, pretty much all ringers of the younger generation were on it, whether or not they were looking for love. Twitter and Facebook had lost something of their edge over time, given all of the non-ringing-related stuff you had to wade through on them. With Ringr, on the other hand, everything was focused on ringing needs, and you could do anything and everything imaginable: hook up with your dream partner, bitch about other people's bells, book an expert to come and tighten up a chamfered bush, or even order four post-peal lamb jalfrezis and a crate of Ludlow Gold to be brought straight to your tower door by a Bulgarian on the back of his moped.

Crispin monitored the little bell icon next to Dom's profile picture obsessively. If it was green, it meant he was online. If he was online, it meant he was available to chat, i.e. not switched off, not asleep or, most importantly, not at some other tower without a mobile signal, ringing something that Crispin couldn't yet do, like Belfast... not ringing it with some of the countless twenty-something spray-tanned muscle men who had cottoned on to ringing and pushed the weaklings like Crispin to the back of the queue. So Crispin took Dom's green bell as a green light to bombard him with needy instant messages:

Penny for your thoughts? {smiley face emoji}

That Glasgow the other night was superb - I wish I could do that LOL {several bell emojis + laughing emoji + crying emoji and/or crying-laughing emoji}

Are you there? ... {puzzled face emoji}

{worried face emoji}

{crying emoji x 3}

The crying emojis would then be deployed liberally at five-minute intervals until Dom replied with something non-committal like *Fine* or *Thanks,* which he never embellished with a smiley face emoji or an *x*, let alone an *xxx*, much to Crispin's chagrin.

Crispin was just in the process of sending Dom a string of zany-face emojis by way of distracting him from his conversation with Sally - nobody having yet managed to invent a convincing stop-talking-to-*her*-and-notice-*me* emoji - when his little attention-seeking plan was rudely interrupted.

"Crispin!" squawked his mother like a chicken with an egg stuck. "Give it a bit of elbow grease! You'll never cool me down properly with that limp wrist of yours."

He flushed crimson and glanced around to see the reaction of other ringers to this embarrassing outburst. Most of them were tactfully trying to ignore it, empathising fully with his predicament: if ever there was an example of someone who deserved full pity for not having been able to choose his family, it was Crispin.

He had usually, however, managed to give himself a

measure of freedom by shuffling Dympna off to the learners' practice run by Frank and Moira Cartlidge over at Clungefunton. He had told her that it would be better for her. *"I'll drop you off on my way to Frotting and pick you up when I'm done. You'll fit in much better at Clungefunton in the early stages,"* had been his argument, *"and then you can come and try your hand at Frotting when you've built up a bit of technique and confidence."*

Little did she realise that her son was being utterly disingenuous. Far from being an easy set of five bells on which to learn, Clungefunton's ring was renowned far and wide for its dreadfulness. Cobbled together in 1946 by conmen who salvaged them in the dead of night from bombed out churches, the bells were horribly mismatched, out of tune, prone to dropping and plagued by weak-shafted, sticky clappers. The entry on the HDGB website summed it up with unequivocal brutality: *"You will never find a more wretched five of scum and villainy."* If Clungefunton couldn't prevent Dympna from making enough progress to make the Frotting grade, then nowhere could. And just to make absolutely sure that his mother would never catch up, Crispin did some additional Machiavellian work behind the scenes to get everyone at Frotting moving on to more advanced things. A little word now and then to Derek so that he wouldn't let the grass grow under Veronica's Reverse Canterbury Pleasure Place… a lavishing of praise for Muriel after a particularly well-controlled bit of handling… a whispered suggestion to Mike that he should maybe blow his own trumpet a bit more in regard to his Battered Sausage. All of these little initiatives would help to keep Frotting moving inexorably onwards and upwards, and to keep his mother way down there at Level 1.

In all honesty though, wherever she went to learn, Dympna was never going to master ringing. She couldn't even remember the right terminology, let alone the technique. Crispin cringed inwardly as he listened in to her describing her current difficulties to Veronica, Phyllis and Muriel...

"I never have any trouble with bell starts…" she announced.

"I think she means 'pulling off'," Veronica whispered to a confused Phyllis.

"...but with bell ends, I don't know whether I'm coming or going. It just keeps bouncing off and I can never get the bloody thing to stop! But I can't get the time to practise it at Clungefunton. You get weekly one-to-ones with Derek, don't you, Muriel? Do you think he might give me one some time?"

It was now dawning on Crispin that his little Clungefunton ruse was already coming apart at the seams and that his mother would not be prevented from going ringing whenever and wherever she so chose, seemingly oblivious - or indifferent - to the fact that she was about as welcome as a prostitute in a nunnery.

"He's a good boy, really, my Crispin," Dympna was saying to Veronica as he tuned back in to eavesdrop on the conversation. "Knows how to look after his mother. Always taking me out for treats. Booked us in for lunch at one of those gastric pubs the other day. My word, it was posh! You could have your eggs cooked for hours at a time in a low-temperature water bath. Reminded me of my menopause…"

Here we go again, thought Crispin. The unpleasant reality of it hit home to him: he did spend too much time with his mother. How ever could he get to know Dominic better if he was to be shackled to her forever more? As far as she was concerned, her son had just not met the right girl yet, and provided that he never did, then everything was wonderful. Cripsin, meanwhile, was fully aware that he had met the right boy and all that needed to happen was for the boy to realise it, and whisk him away to a life of rural domestic bliss, with Springer Spaniels, hanging baskets, Eurovision box-sets, a solid-fuel Aga and a whopping great chamber organ.

Crispin had always wanted to learn the organ, having been a keyboard enthusiast since childhood; he was Grade 7 piano and had even built up his own small collection of assorted diminutive members of the keyboard family over the years, a hobby made possible via his mother's heavy involvement in the antiques trading scene. Celeste, clavicytherium, spinet, pianola, virginal… you name it, Crispin had an example of it, although most of them were relatively cheap modern reproductions and they sat gathering dust in what was once the playroom. In fact, the instruments had become as much Dympna's problem as Crispin's. She couldn't resist the urge to spoil him, basically. She would buy him faux-medieval spinets in the way that most mothers bought their sons packets of their favourite Maryland cookies, or six-packs of M&S boxer shorts, just in case they were running out. Barely a month went by in which she did not appear back home from Philip Serrell's Auction House with yet another harpsichord squeezed into the back of her Honda Jazz.

"Another one, Mother?" Crispin would ask, almost in exasperation. "I think I've got that one already anyway."

"Ooh, I couldn't resist," she would reply. "Beat off an archdeacon from Powys who was bidding against me, but still it came in under the estimate. Bit of a restoration job for you to stop you getting bored. I know how much you like to get down to a good bit of French polishing. You'll have to lift it out yourself, though. I felt something go twinge while I was helping Philip to shove it in."

All of these instrumental acquisitions, amassed so carefully over the years, sadly paled in comparison to that which Crispin now desired. It was the organ, and the mastery thereof, for which he desperately yearned. Not that he didn't get his fair share of organ action, if the truth be told. He could stand in for church services if required, and did so on a regular basis in and around the local area, often at Clungefunton, when Ruth Gillon-Smith was away for the weekend with her ladies' rambling group slogging through another chunk of Offa's Dyke. However, the plethora of knobs got him in all of a kerfuffle and he would always just pull out a random selection and hope for the best. He longed for Dominic to give him a full masterclass at Granser, to explain all the ins and outs, and let him have a go on his 16-foot wood. For Crispin, just plink-plonking away at home on his overused Bechstein upright no longer cut the mustard.

But Dominic just kept refusing to take the hint and seemed oblivious to the real intent behind Crispin's bids for his attention. He just seemed to shrug them all off and stuck firmly to his usual one-track mind, way up there in the virtuoso organists' stratosphere, a place that he was perfectly content to explore unaccompanied. He had no time to take a lacklustre intermediate like Crispin in hand, and no interest in messing about with twinkly little virginals and the like. That was the harsh reality of it. There he was, chatting away happily with Sally about his little Welsh jaunt, and Crispin eavesdropped with mounting jealousy on all his vivid descriptions of Gemshorns, Dulcianas and Open Diapasons.

"…Oh, and Y Llanasnart…" he was telling her with trembling excitement, "Now that really was a revelation. Such a beautiful Clarabella, and the way the Oboe speaks - gorgeous, simply gorgeous. The depth and penetration of the 8-foot Horn would make your hair stand on end, it really would. Plus, to cap it all, it's got the biggest original Swell to Great stop knob in the country. I could have died and gone to heaven!"

How come Dominic got to have such a glamorous life, independently wealthy and free to be effectively a gentleman of leisure? Dominic's weekly 'work' entailed playing for two or three Sunday services, with the occasional wedding or funeral thrown in to top up his pocket money. And no matter how much he spent on aftershave and weekends in Dorset, he still always seemed to have a thousand or two left over to invest in random unnecessary modifications to his BMW. Life was so unfair!

Crispin, by contrast, had to slave away from nine to five, six days a week, desperately trying to squeeze whatever commission he could out of gullible middle-class customers for inexplicably complicated thermostatic mixer taps. He had worked as a

'Bathroom Design Representative' for three years now, 'Salesman' being considered too 'in your face' for the modern customer (or 'end consumer', as his boss and fellow ringer of long standing, Fleet Carr, insisted that they be called.) The holidays and pay were reasonable when compared to the competition, it was true, and the overtime was not that onerous, but there was no getting away from the fact that Crispin was seriously underchallenged at Granser Sinks. The only thing he looked forward to about the place was the several hours of respite it provided from Dympna's incessant litany of woe on such fascinating topics as the irreparable damage his huge foetal cranium had done to her symphysis pubis. At least Mr Carr going on about client conversion targets could wash over him like white noise, and he could sit there looking like he was paying attention. With his mother, on the other hand, there was just no practical way of blocking it out when bombarded at full volume with the graphic minutiae of yet another uterine prolapse on the Debenhams escalator.

"Don't look so glum!" Fleet would say to Crispin to chivvy him up whilst he was staring vacantly out at the passing traffic on Granser High Street. "You'll never get your monthly quota of steam showers shifted if you just sit there with a face like a bag of muffles. The clientele will not part with their cash when all you do is convey the atmosphere of a Stalinist sanatorium in downtown Minsk."

"I'll try…" replied Crispin, not really trying at all.

"Besides," continued Fleet, "isn't it Frotting tonight? You've got that to look forward to, haven't you?"

"I suppose so."

"I think I might join you. I haven't seen Bev for a few weeks at the Granser practice, and I want to tell her my good news…"

Bev Belleau was very definitely on Fleet Carr's radar, and had been ever since the pair of them met several years previously at a Stedman Caters special practice in Shrewsbury. She had been married at the time, of course, but Fleet liked a challenge, and the more he encouraged her to come away for the weekend to mess about with The Rector's Ring and suchlike, the more he managed to drive a wedge between Bev and Chester Belleau. Conveniently enough, the less that Chester saw of Bev, the less he missed her, and he ultimately came to the conclusion that he did not love her. He loved snooker, Sudokus and silence. And so, by and large amicably, they went their separate ways, with Bev getting the house and Chester taking a suitcase of clothes, the tropical fish and the Volvo.

However, even though she had been single again for as long as Fleet could remember, Bev did not succumb to his advances. She joined him for quarters and peals, of course, attending whatever tower grabs he decided to set up for the Granser crowd, and always proving that she was more than able to handle a big one. She even dealt with the Great Bell of Tong with panache and aplomb, jumping up onto the box and getting on with it to the envy of those fellow ringers who would never dream of handling something of such immense weight.

"Now, this is a real honour," Fleet told her before they got started. "You have to be a bloody good ringer before you can get given Tong. If they don't think you can get it up, you won't get a look in. There are some who've been waiting for years, and for most of them it'll sadly never happen!"

"I'll do my best," said Bev, almost trembling with excitement at the prospect.

"It's seriously heavy," he warned. "It might lift you off your feet. Do you think you might be better off with a strap on?"

"No," scoffed Bev. "I can manage it *au naturel*. Just you watch!"

And she did. Fleet had never seen such consummate handling, and it made him desire her all the more. He wanted to compose new methods with her and give them names, like children. He dropped enough hints, and even showed her some initial rough workings. However, she still remained coy, and every time it looked as if she might be persuaded to come round after closing time for an evening of exploratory pricking in the back office at Granser Sinks, she always seemed to have some kind of excuse. Fleet wondered if she was maybe intimidated by his status as a freemason, a benefactor to good causes and a leading light in the local business fraternity. For all of the body confidence that her choice of stretch fabrics conveyed to the onlooker, her self-esteem was altogether more fragile, hence her tendency to take things so personally when her fellow ringers made it clear that they did not want their ringing room painted in pustulant pink. How would she react, wondered Fleet, when he announced to her that he was soon to be knighted for services to bathroom sophistication? Beverley and Sir Fleet... What a couple they would make! Similar in so many ways... they were made for each other! And yet, Fleet Carr's mood was a mix of exhilaration and trepidation. Would she fling herself into his arms or collapse in a heap of self-conscious inadequacy? He would have to tread carefully. But, one way or another, however long it took, Fleet would make Beverley his very own…

It was just as Crispin was moping on the injustice of his daily drudgery at Granser Sinks that the primary cause of it marched in through the door. Fleet Carr, resplendent in Michael Portillo candy-floss chinos and Paisley cravat, announced his presence with a policemanly "Evening, all!" and made an immediate beeline for the semi-empty bench space next to Bev. Phyllis budged up to let him squish in and was instantly intrigued by the scent of his aftershave.

"I'm sure I recognise that," she said to him. "Brut for Men, by any chance?"

"Hardly," he replied, trying not to scoff. "Penhaligons." He presented her with his cuff so she could have a quick sniff.

"Aren't Penhaligons biscuits?"

"That's Penguins, you silly mare!" interjected Veronica. "Can't take her anywhere."

"I know what a Penguin is, Veronica. I'm talking about those posh ones, like Prince Charles makes…" And off they went into a topic that at least made a welcome change from the usual flower arranging and PCC controversies.

With Phyllis now preoccupied with searching her mental filing cabinet for the particular biscuit brand that refused to pop up and make itself known, Fleet turned to Bev. She was busily scrutinising her Twatt, keen to get to grips with what was going on at the front, as well as in the numerous awkward places.

"Twatt Bob Major!" said Fleet. "Wow! I've been trying to get Twatt for heaven knows how long now. I came so close the other week with some of the Nottingham University lot, but it fired out five minutes before the end. Such a disappointment!"

"Well, we've been going at it a couple of times already too," said Bev in a tone of tired resignation. "Harder to work your way around than you might imagine. You just think you've got to grips with it and then - boom! - it's all gone belly up. If you want to be in it this time, though, you only have to ask. It was completely full up, as I understand it, but I've a feeling one or two have dropped out. Technically, though, it's Hazel's Twatt, so you'd better ask her."

"When is it?"

"A week on Friday. 7 pm."

"Damn!" exclaimed Fleet, staring in disappointment

at his online calendar. "I'm down to help out with a touch of Slack Bottom that evening. I'll see if I can get out of it. I don't mind a bit of Slack Bottom if I'm otherwise kicking my heels, but it's hardly in the same league as Twatt now, is it?"

"I'd have preferred to have a stab at Dancing Dicks, if I'm brutally honest," confessed Bev, "but Hazel's a bit of a stickler for first-things-first. She's not going to move on until she's got Twatt in the bag, and that's all there is to it."

"Understandable," said Fleet, and then, changing the subject, with a smile but also a tone that conveyed a certain gravitas, "I have some good news, by the way." He had resolved not to beat about the bush and just get it over with, confident ultimately that Bev could handle the magnitude of his revelation.

"Oh yes?" said Bev, feigning the usual coyness. *(She was such a bloody flirt!)*

"I've been invited to the palace…" - Bev's eyes widened at this - "…and I'm going to be knighted for services to bathroom sophistication."

"Knighted?" Bev was virtually dumbfounded. "*Sir* Fleet?"

"The very same," he confirmed.

"Oh, how wonderful!" Bev threw her arms around him. "Everyone, listen while Fleet tells you his news!"

And on hearing his story, all of the assembled gave a hearty round of applause and slapped him on the back. Here they were, in the company of the man whose greatness was to ensure that the wider world would finally have heard of Granser! Crowds would flock to the place and come to stare in wonder at Granser Sinks, amazed that such beauty and business prowess could have stemmed from such humble beginnings. (Fleet was the seventh child of a local pig slurry delivery man, the full rags-to-riches account of which would soon be known to sentimental *Midlands Today* viewers everywhere.)

Yes, Granser finally had its own home-grown hero and they applauded all the more loudly in celebration. All except Crispin, that is, who made a show of congratulation for the benefit of the present company, but who had been dreading the imminent increased inflation of his boss' ego. (Having a passing acquaintance with Fleet Carr was one thing; dealing with him 9 to 5, Monday to Friday, plus most Saturday mornings and during overtime was a different kettle of fish altogether...) He would be insufferable from now on, not only droning on about monthly target strategies for after-sales client care packages, but also trying to explain the concept of half-leads during mid-morning coffee breaks in a condescending *'I'm-a-Sir-now'* type of voice.

When would the world take Crispin seriously? His boss thought he was a nobody; his mother thought he was still stuck halfway out of her birth canal; and Dom, dear sweet dishy Dom, who knew what he thought? If Crispin had been an organ, Dom wouldn't be able to keep his hands off him, but what was the point of having such fruitless pipe dreams? No, if Crispin wanted to be noticed, he would have to break free of the ties that bound him, throw caution to the wind and be, for want of a better word, *a man*!

"Stop biting your nails!"

Dympna's screeched command jolted Crispin out of his momentary epiphany, and turning on the spur of the moment to say: *"Mind your own fucking business!"* he actually said "Sorry…" and retreated back inside the shell that suddenly felt more like home than ever.

"Just like his father…" continued Dympna to Veronica and Phyllis, extrapolating her pet theory of how glaring inadequacies always get passed down the line from Capricorn men to Virgo sons with Uranus rising.

"I know what you mean," nodded Phyllis. "My Eric's a Capricorn and he's a waste of space too. Sits there with the cricket on. Won't try anything new. I try sending him out to do little things in the garden, but ultimately, he's clueless…"

She was on a roll now, with Dympna and Veronica hanging on her every word, frowning and tutting in heartfelt sympathy.

"…He can't even find my clematis," she continued, "let alone bring it back to life! It's sitting there all dry and withered, but he pays it no attention whatsoever."

"Sounds like my Jim," agreed Veronica. "Never had green fingers. He just whips out whatever tool comes to hand and goes at it like a bull in a china shop. To him, a bush is a bush is a bush. Gives it the five-minute once over when it starts to get straggly and then it's completely forgotten about for the rest of the year. No finesse whatsoever…"

"Oh, well, Crispin's father's very much in his element in the garden, admittedly," butted in Dympna. "Out there for hours at a time fiddling about trying to get his peonies to stay upright. Crispin pops out to give him a hand now and then too, don't you, chicken?"

Crispin started wondering if his mood could possibly get any worse and perhaps the only option left open to him now would be to stand up and storm out. His thoughts of escape were stopped in their tracks, however, by the appearance of a dark shadow in the doorway. Stepping forward into the light in steely silence, finally there she was: Bertha Gorse…

Bertha was a small woman. Birdlike, you might say, but whilst the outer shell was sparrow, the heart was pure vulture. She glared around the room as she stepped into it, her gaze instinctively focusing upon anything immediately and obviously identifiable as a Health and Safety issue. Was that curtain fire retardant? Had that carpet been properly tacked down? Was that Henry's PAT test up to date? You could see the multiple disastrous scenarios in her mind revealing themselves in the narrowing of her eyes and the tightening purse of her thin, dry lips. And this was before she'd even said a word...

"Good evening!" Bertha finally announced with the ominous drama of that newsreader who always gets to tell the world of Kim Jong-Un's latest triumph. Semi-breathless, she plonked her dripping tartan shopping trolley down next to her with a telling thud. Everybody knew from legend what it must contain: the twelve infamous leather-bound volumes of the BREASts Health and Safety Policy...

"Good evening, Ms Gorse," everyone replied sullenly in unison like naughty school children awaiting the full details of their imminent punishment.

"Oh, call me Bertha," she insisted, removing her headscarf to reveal the hairstyle that everyone knew so well from her photo on the CCCCCCR website: a neatly styled but ultimately very plain bob. "I may be here on official business, but we can dispense with those kinds of formalities. First names never killed anybody… Well, not yet, as far as I know! Hazel, I understand you are the current tower captain, is that correct?"

"Yes, Bertha," replied Hazel nervously, her whole body visibly trembling as she reached out to shake Bertha's hand.

"We don't shake hands anymore," said Bertha brusquely. "You should know that. Did you not read Directive H348/04?"

"Yes, of course. Sorry…"

"A simple hello will suffice."

"Hello, Bertha," muttered Hazel, kicking herself for having already got off to a shaky start. "I hope you are well. I saw you on Bellboard last week, actually. That 720 of Plain Bob you rang the treble for, to celebrate your niece's Grade 3 Oboe Merit. Well done on that!" This was very definitely the wrong thing to say. Bertha looked suddenly incandescent with rage.

"That's the other Bertha Gorse, Bertha *F* Gorse! The one from Stourport who'd struggle to ring a doorbell. I'm Bertha *N J* Gorse, and I can ring 8-spliced double-handed, I'll have you know."

"I'm so sorry," spluttered Hazel.

"Not to worry," replied Bertha, pursing her lips into a full cat's arse. "I wouldn't expect people in an insignificant backwater like Frotting to know my ringing record. Now, let's get down to business. It shouldn't take long and once the relevant boxes are ticked, I'll be able to sign you off as 'Requires Improvement', or maybe even 'Satisfactory', but let's not get our hopes up just yet."

Veronica, Phyllis and Muriel immediately set to whispering to each other about what grade they thought Frotting would get, or more to the point, what it in reality deserved. The general consensus amongst the three of them was that the shoddy hemming of the balcony curtain would surely get a black mark and that Hazel and Derek's consistent failure to raise the question of heating with the vicar would put them into dangerous territory.

"Shush!" Bertha hissed, to castigate them for their rudeness. "There is to be no irrelevant chattering during the assessment. Rules are rules!"

As Bertha glanced down to the first sheet on her clipboard, the ladies rolled their eyes and passed around the Quality Street in grudging silence.

"Stop!" screeched Bertha. "I can hear rustling! What is it?"

"Quality Street," replied Phyllis with an edge of insolence to her voice. "Would you like one?"

"What?!" gasped Bertha, and turning to Hazel with an accusatory glare. "That's not in the last risk assessment that you submitted to me."

"It never occurred to me!" quailed Hazel. "Is there a problem?"

"Nuts!" bellowed Bertha, seizing the box and pointing to the label. "Nuts! Nuts! Nuts!"

"Oh, everybody knows which Quality Street to avoid if they have a nut allergy," scoffed Muriel. "They can just have a toffee penny, and like it or lump it, can't they?"

"That's a very cavalier assumption, if I may say so," retorted Bertha indignantly. "Visiting ringers may never have come across Quality Street in their lives. If they're from the Surrey Association, for example, they may only be familiar with Organic Green & Blacks or Hotel Chocolat 70% Dark Fair-Trade

Batons. Have you thought about that? Just because the Hereford Guild is still living in the dark ages where tower treats are concerned doesn't mean everybody else is! No, I'm sorry, but they're going to have to go." With that, Bertha put a big red tick in her 'Identified Risk' box, snapped on her latex gloves, poured the Quality Street into a yellow biohazard bag and plonked them outside on the stairs where they could pose no further threat.

"I broke my tooth on a Murray Mint in Sainsbury's car park once," piped up Dympna by way of breaking the awkward silence. "You can never be too careful…"

"Where's the hand sanitizer?" asked Bertha, ignoring Dympna's little intervention.

Derek fished the dispenser out from the odds-and-ends cupboard and surreptitiously tried to remove some of the dust that had already accumulated on it since it got put away back in early 2021. He pumped it vigorously over Bertha's cupped hands, but nothing came. He gave it a good shake and tried again. Still nothing.

"Oh, for heaven's sake!" scolded Bertha. "It must be completely dried up."

"Give it a moment," urged Derek. "It's nearly there! Yes, yes, I can feel it. It's coming!"

And with that, a tiny congealed blob, slightly yellowed with age, plopped pathetically into Bertha's open palm.

"Obviously past its use-by date," she declared, and made another red mark on her clipboard with a deliberately flamboyant flourish. "Hygiene is the cornerstone of a safe and happy tower. I need hardly remind you of those slaphappy towers with unrestrained members that had to be sealed off and fumigated during the COVID outbreak," said Bertha sternly. "Nottingham All Saints, Garlickhythe, Burley St Matthias, Sandbach, Chester Cathedral… Need I go on? But what can you expect when reckless individuals go around handling each other's tail ends willy-nilly!"

Everybody did their best to look contrite at the slapdash approach to Frotting hand hygiene that Bertha had identified and Bev volunteered to pick up a fresh bottle at Tesco first thing in the morning.

"Before I move on," said Bertha, using a wet wipe to get rid of the mess with which Derek had left her, "I'm going to need to confirm that you have an Epipen in situ. If there have been nuts in the ringing room, which there clearly have, then you fall into the category of requiring provision for the treatment of anaphylactic shock. The half-life of nut dust, might I add, is thought to be in the region of eighty years, so you're going to need at least one Epipen to live in your first aid kit well into the next century."

"What's an Epipen?" whispered Muriel to Dom and Sally sheepishly, thinking that they looked young and trendy enough to know that kind of thing.

"An adrenaline injector," explained Dom. "You stab it into someone's leg and it brings them back from the dead, basically."

You could do with one of them every week, Muriel, thought Sally, without actually saying so. *Might get you to ring the bloody bell up properly.*

Bertha inspected the Epipen that Hazel had fished out from the first aid kit under the tower table, checking the all-important use-by date.

"It's acceptable," she announced, "but only just. You'll need another one in October." She ticked it off the list begrudgingly, placing it back on the table, and Hazel breathed a visible sigh of relief. The only reason that they had the Epipen at all was that it had been forgotten by one of the Leicester Rising Ringers who turned up on a ringing tour before lockdown. His particular allergy had been to shellfish, which everyone thankfully found out about just before Muriel fished out her buttered mussel fancies in the tea break.

"I'll be back in November to confirm that you have replaced it," continued Bertha, "and I will see to it personally that the out-of-date one is destroyed." (Bertha liked the word 'destroyed'. She always put special emphasis upon it and her eyes lit up whenever it came out of her mouth.) She moved onto the next item on her clipboard. "Now, let me see the emergency evacuation procedure."

"Oh yes," said Hazel excitedly. "We've got this one nailed. Shoes off and all loose objects over here, everybody!" An assortment of oddments cascaded onto the tower table in rapid succession: false teeth, spectacles, ancient folded up bits of paper with plain hunt written out on them by hand, mobile phones, Bev's Estee Lauder lipstick, Derek's metal fid and an appliance that Crispin would rather other people didn't know about. (He kept it in a drawstring leatherette pouch, though, so unless someone went poking around, everyone would be thankfully none the wiser…) As everyone patted their pockets and other areas of their person for things that might have slipped through the net, Hazel moved over to the switches behind the curtain for the big reveal.

 "Stand back!"

And with that, she set off the amber klaxon and pressed the big red button to deploy the rubber evacuation slide. It thrust itself out instantaneously from the ringing room balcony and flopped down onto the nave like the tongue of a giant yellow chameleon.

"And jump! And jump! And jump!"

One by one, the ringers crossed their arms over their chests and hurled themselves onto the slide, zooming down to the safety of the ground floor below.

"I assume you don't need me to go down too?" Hazel asked Bertha as she chivvied everyone on in turn.

"No," confirmed Bertha. "That's quite alright. I'm sure you'd know what to do in a real situation."

"Go on," said Hazel to Crispin finally, who was nervous of heights. "Take up the rear." And with a bit of a shove, he was on his way, screaming in momentary terror.

"Not bad," said Bertha. "Not bad. Full evacuation in twenty-three seconds. There aren't many towers that can boast that kind of efficiency. You've clearly been practising!"

"We like to try," replied Hazel modestly.

"And I'm impressed that you managed to get a faculty for such a modern innovation!"

"Oh, well, friends in high places," whispered Hazel with a wink. "The bishop's brother does a roaring trade dismantling British Airways' old 747s over near Abergavenny, so he was able to get us a good deal, and no questions asked. He even threw in some bits of fuselage for free so that we can patch up the holes in the tower roof."

"Very clever," said Bertha. The ringers were now making their way back up the tower stairs as the escape slide deflated itself and slowly retreated back into its lair with a laryngitic wheeze. As soon as they were all back inside and installed on the benches, Bertha continued: "Now, back to hygiene. What are we doing about the ropes? How are we avoiding cross-contamination?"

An awkward silence, during which everybody secretly acknowledged that they'd skipped over that bit in the risk assessment.

"We've got some Marigolds in the kitchen," piped up Veronica finally in an attempt to be helpful.

Bertha gave her a vicious look. "I hardly think bringing rubber gloves back and forth between the kitchen and the ringing room is best practice, now, is it? We've already seen that you're falling way below the mark on the sanitiser front..." (Derek shuffled uncomfortably at this and looked at his feet.) "...and I doubt that you're all going up and down the stairs to wash your hands between touches. Presumably, then, you're all just sticking to your own rope throughout?"

"Yes, that's right," Hazel lied. She did a quick mental calculation as to how she and Derek could possibly make this work, given that there were more than eight of them at the practice. Well, Phyllis, Veronica and Muriel would be quite happy to sit out all night and catch up on the gossip that they'd missed out on throughout August in regard to the flower-arranging rota war which had been raging for years, and for which peace talks had thus far failed to elicit even a temporary ceasefire. They could also thrash out the details surrounding the vicar's insistence that if the young mothers wanted to do Messy Church on a regular basis, then there would also have to be a monthly liturgical kindergarten, complete with 40-minute sermon, to balance things out. (The vicar was circumspect about the ethics that underlay the concept of Messy Church, by all accounts, and put particularly strong emphasis upon his disapproval of Soft Play within an ecclesiastical setting.) As long as Hazel announced that they weren't going to ring Rounds and Call Changes or Grandsire Doubles this evening, then the ladies would take the hint, fish out their crochet work and get busy with the bitching.

"Actually," said Bertha. "We do have a new innovation that enables the use of different ropes during a single practice, and I'm looking for guinea pigs to see how it might work."

"Oh, really?" interjected Mike, suddenly perking up at the mention of something that might enable more ringing to happen. (His withdrawal symptoms were kicking in, it being already ten-to-eight and no sign of the practice getting underway any time soon.) "Do show us!"

Bertha crouched down to rummage in her trolley and out it came, a strangely familiar object sealed in foil, only somewhat bigger than anyone had seen before, even Dom. Bertha tore it open and held the contents aloft for all to see. "It's a latex rope protector, in case you were wondering," she announced, the retired biology teacher coming into her own as she proceeded to demonstrate. "Simply grasp the tail end firmly in one hand and the protector in the other, squeezing the tip to ensure that no air can get in. Then, maintaining your grip and pulling the rope taut, unroll the protector up and over the entire length of the sally. This can take some getting used to, as the viricidal jelly can be a bit slippery at first, but you'll soon get the knack, and, hey presto! You can practice safe ringing to your heart's content."

"Are they single use, then?" asked Bev.

"Of course they are!" snapped Bertha. "Each ringer needs to carry their own supply and use a fresh one every time they come into contact with a new rope. After ringing, they need to be wrapped up in tissue paper and placed in the bin. They are *not*, I repeat, *not* flushable!" She rolled the slimy sheath back down the rope and held it aloft for all to see, before safely encasing it in a few sheets of Cushelle and dropping it into another of her ubiquitous biohazard bags. "I will use my own hand sanitizer this time, I think." And she made a deliberate point of highlighting the superiority of her own personal alcohol gel by making it fire out in a spectacular fluid jet at the merest touch of her pump-action dispenser. "Would anybody else like some?"

Everyone felt duly obliged to hold forth their hands as if in readiness to receive the host, and Bertha went round the circle efficiently squirting out her magical elixir.

"Excellent," she declared as they all rubbed their hands to get rid of the unpleasant gooey feel. "All safe again now. Now how are you getting on with your RIPs?" Ringing Isolation Pods were the next item on her list and Bertha was keen to establish that all of the towers in her jurisdiction were planning ahead for the arrival of the next killer virus, whenever it may materialise.

"We've just got the one in place so far, I'm afraid, Bertha," explained Hazel, "as we'll need a few more fundraisers before we can get another £5,000 for the next one. Muriel's annual September Sausage Party at Swan Cottage should bring in a good profit though. Derek, if you could take the tenor so we can demonstrate..." Hazel flicked the lever that set the mechanism whirring and everybody watched as the inch-thick Perspex tube descended smoothly from the ceiling to encase Derek like a zoological specimen. Its diameter left just enough room for free movement and Derek rang the tenor halfway up and back down again to show that the system was clearly going to work just fine.

"Say a few words," said Hazel, who was keen to show that the ticket kiosk intercom system embedded in the tube at mouth height was fully operational.

"Such as?" asked Derek, embarrassedly.

"Just something that you'd normally say in the course of a typical practice."

"Erm…" said Derek, trying to think. "Oh, yes, I've got it! *For Christ's sake, Veronica, it's places in Reverse Canterbury, not dodges! How many bloody times?!*" The volume on the intercom system was certainly impressive, and but for a bit of the crackling you might expect, Derek's booming commandment could be heard loud and clear as it echoed off the stone walls. Veronica even looked like she'd actually listened too for a change.

"Very good," said Bertha with a smile of satisfaction. "I can tick that off the list." And she did so with a flamboyant stroke of her biro that skidded off the page and across the underlying copy of the Frotting risk assessment. "Damn!" she cursed. "I've spoiled that good and proper now..."

"Not to worry," said Hazel. "Take one of ours." She pointed to a pile of fifteen pristine, unread copies in the dustiest corner of the ringing room. Then, realising that she had put her foot in it, she covered her tracks with the stammered explanation that she always printed out extras for visiting bands.

"Thinking ahead! Very wise, very wise... I suggest that you release Mr Beavis now, by the way." Bertha had observed him tapping gently on the Perspex through the corner of her eye and thought he might be getting a bit hot under the collar in there, what with the extra warmth provided by his tightly-hoisted knee-high terylene SACY socks and v-neck jumper.

As Hazel turned away to trigger the raising of Derek's pod, Bertha applied another squirt of alcohol gel before going to collect one of the spare risk assessments. Tutting, she indicated something long, brown and furry stretched out under the bookcase: "Who would leave their coat on the floor like that? Trip hazard!" She stooped to pick it up, whereupon it rolled over, barked and gave her hand a luscious, slobbery lick.

"Dog!" screamed Bertha in disgust, her face transformed to a Greek tragedy mask. "Dog!"

"Hastings! Stay!" commanded Hazel. Hastings duly ignored her and, clearly enamoured, rose up on his hind legs to present Bertha with his quivering, crimson lipstick.

"Aaaargh!" shrieked the object of his affections, holding her hands up, frozen in a pose of concrete horror. "Get it off me! Get it off me!"

"He's just being friendly," stammered Hazel, dashing over to pull him off. But before she could get there, Bertha's paralysis was broken and she made an instinctive dash for the stairs, wailing, her deep-seated fear of dogs driving her flight response. And it was this that triggered a chain of events that would not be forgotten for a very long time…

The first casualty was Bertha's alcohol gel. In her uncontrolled bid for escape, it flew out of her hand, landed on top of the risk assessments and poured out over them. (Bertha had left the screw top loose - naughty!) From there, it proceeded to drip down onto the Dimplex, which was still switched on underneath the bench. The inevitable happened. The Dimplex gave off a dazzling blue-ish spark followed by an almighty bang. This minor explosion proceeded to set the risk assessments on fire, which, thanks to the added alcohol, began to burn fiercely within seconds. Mike's nearby cagoule was just what the fire wanted, of course, and that too took flame like the legendary burning bush.

"Fire!" yelled Fleet, stating the obvious, in an attempt to show the leadership skills one would expect of a future knight of the realm. "Hazel! Evacuation procedure, I think!" Hazel, recovering from the momentary shock of the situation, acquired a clear head and once again triggered the inflatable slide, which spat itself out into the nave as before.

Bertha, by contrast, continued to panic in post-dog trauma, ignoring all of her training which would have told her to keep calm. She continued to head for the door, knocking the tower table clean over in the process. This particular calamity sent the Epipen flying through the air, and, like the sword of Damocles, it fell onto the slide, piercing it instantly, just as Dympna and Phyllis had crossed their arms across their chests to take the plunge. Farting like an elephant on a broccoli diet, the slide came free from its moorings and whizzed around the body of the church, bouncing off the walls, taking the ladies on a magic-carpet ride from hell. It finally dumped them in flabby lumps, just in front of the altar, like fallen angels in M&S knitwear.

"Don't move, ladies!" Mike shouted up to the injured parties, who were groaning and trembling on the altar steps. "We'll be with you as soon as we can! Once this fire's out, we'll be able to get down the stairs!"

"My arm!" wailed Phyllis, gripping the useless, misshapen limb, which would not be kneading any more fig and All Bran cookie dough for many a month to come. (Her husband's lower intestine would just have to make do with alternative arrangements for the foreseeable.)

Dympna, for her part, was uncharacteristically silent, such was the shock of the fall and its immediate repercussions. The substandard repair to her pelvic floor had finally succumbed to wet rot and it had come away completely at the skirting boards. Unwilling to risk getting up for fear of what she might leave sitting there on the altar steps, she obeyed Mike's instruction and remembered the gynaecologist's wise, wise words: *If in doubt, clench!*

Meanwhile, the fire continued to rage, adding Bev's fake leopard skin and Dom's nylon Rab jacket to its list of easily-digestible victims. One by one, the coats lined up on the hooks were headed for a similar fate, but luckily, Fleet had located the fire extinguisher, safely hidden in a boxful of polystyrene Quavers behind the nylon acetate balcony curtain. He called upon Crispin to help him read the instructions, having left his glasses in the glovebox of the Audi, and they set to work finally with the task of bringing the fire under control. The extinguisher did a surprisingly efficient job, given that it had last been checked over when Florence Nightingale was still on the ten-pound note. A few well-directed blasts and Fleet had it out in no time.

Suddenly, seemingly out of nowhere, lightning flashed all around the ringing room and everyone realised that, in all of the panic, the worsening of the storm outside had completely passed them by.

Furthermore, where was Bertha? Bev and Sally narrowed their eyes to try and spot her through the haze of smoke, but she was nowhere to be seen.

Then Bev spotted one sorry shoe on the top tower step…

It didn't take them long to put two and two together. The shopping trolley containing the BREASts Health and Safety policy was on its side nearby. Clearly Bertha had tripped over it in her mad dash to escape and fallen down the spiral staircase! Bev and Sally went down as quickly but as carefully as they could in the smoggy darkness, and there, at the bottom of the stairs in a tangle of angular limbs, they found her, quite unconscious.

"She must have slipped on this as well," said Bev, sadly. It was the yellow biohazard bag containing the condemned Quality Street, its torn polythene knotted around Bertha's clearly broken ankle.

Just as Sally started to help Bev straighten out the lumpen mess that was Bertha, Mike squeezed past them en route to see to Phyllis and Dympna, first aid kit in hand. Then out of nowhere, a scream came echoing down the staircase from above…

"Oh my God! Derek!" The voice was Hazel's. "Help me get the pod off him! Quick!"

"You stay with Bertha!" Sally instructed Bev. "I'll go up and help."

Overheated in his SACY uniform, deprived of

sufficient oxygen by both the fire and the isolation pod, and prone to asthma at the best of times, Derek had collapsed to the floor. The lack of space preventing a full prostration, he had ended up slumped uncomfortably, his cheek pressed up against the Perspex, with a colour in them that was not far off that of Muriel's varicose veins.

Hazel was over in the corner, frantically flicking on and off, but couldn't get the switch to respond. "Oh God! Oh God!" she cried. "The fuse must have gone!"

"We'll have to do it ourselves then," said Fleet. "Come on, boys!" So Crispin and Dom joined him around the pod, pressing their palms against the glassy surface to lift it manually up and away from Derek's limp body. Sally crouched down to catch his head and prevent it hitting the floor, a gesture which also had the added bonus of preventing a cloud of his dandruff from becoming airborne to result in further possible breathing complications.

This was the point at which Veronica and Muriel came into their own. Previously all of a dither, their mental processing unable to keep up with the speed at which events had unfolded, their St John's Ambulance training now kicked in and they were suddenly in their element.

"Airway, Breathing, Circulation!" chanted Veronica,

the litany coming back automatically to her like the Nicene Creed.

"We're OK on all three," confirmed Muriel.

Sally nodded in agreement. "Yes, he's still with us. Just."

"Recovery position!" said Veronica, and, helped by Muriel and Sally, they arranged him in the time-honoured way. Veronica completed the procedure by pushing his head right back to keep the airway clear, and finally loosened the belt that was holding up his shorts. (*Is that an official part of the recovery position routine?* Sally wondered, but then she was no expert, so thought it best not to quibble.)

"Now call 999!" instructed Veronica.

Everyone stared back at her in disbelief. Dom even had to suppress a snigger.

"Mobile phone signal?" he scoffed. "You're having a laugh, aren't you? This is Shropshire, not Silicon Valley. Come on, Crispin. We'd better head into the village for help."

Secretly delighted to be called upon for this special privilege, Crispin grabbed the head-to-toe rubber Millets rain poncho and matching gaiters without which Dympna wouldn't let him leave the house if there was a sniff of rain in the forecast. In a trice, he was ready for action, buzzing with adrenaline and fully protected from the threat of unexpected leakage.

"Don't you want to see how your mother is first?" asked Muriel, concerned.

"Do I have to?" asked Crispin, without pausing to think. He glanced over to Dympna, who was clearly back in rude health, explaining to Mike with all manner of horribly familiar gestures just what had happened in the region of her lower abdomen. "I mean, erm, I'm not good with, erm, female matters..." (Mike, of course, would be no better with such things, but rather him than Crispin, quite frankly. At least Mike didn't have to take the grisly details home with him and lie in bed, sleeplessly visualising them at four in the morning.)

"We'd better get going," urged Dom. "We'll take Hastings with us, Hazel. He looks like he could do with some fresh air." Hastings wagged his tail furiously, realising that he was finally about to do something fun, and when he saw Hazel rummaging in the special bag with the harnesses, Bonios and pooper scooper, he positively jumped for joy.

"Here's the long lead," said Hazel, handing it over to Dom. "He'll pull too hard if you're not careful, and he'll want to be out at the front the whole time. Be firm and that should put him back where you want him."

Just as Crispin, Dom and Hastings headed off down the stairs, they were met by the sound of Bev, who was calling up to the others in a panic.

"Bertha's pulse is weakening!" she cried. "We need to do something before we lose her!"

"Quick, boys!" urged Hazel. "You stick to the plan and try to get to a phone in the village. Fleet, you help me get the defibrillator, the heart monitor and the ventilator unpacked!"

What a stroke of luck that the CCCCCCR made us invest in these! thought Hazel as she tore away the sheets of bubble wrap, resisting the temptation to pause and pop a few bubbles for the purposes of stress relief. It had been one of the conditions for a return to normal ringing that your tower would need to have intensive care facilities installed, so, all in all, given the current turn of events, the £35,000 investment had been a wise one. The package also included a spinal immobilisation stretcher and a foldaway hospital bed, which they managed to get set up in the corner behind the tenor in no time. There was even a trolley load of swabs, bandages and other handy oddments that meant they could deal with the minor casualties too.

"Hang on in there, Mrs Hipkiss!" shouted Muriel up the nave to a distinctly soggy-looking Dympna. "We've got pads!" She chucked some over the balcony to Mike, along with a triangular bandage for Phyllis' arm, and he dashed back up the nave to do the necessaries.

Sally and Fleet, meanwhile, managed to get the stretcher down the awkwardly windy staircase, where they helped Bev to load on the now critical-looking Bertha. Whether or not they had managed to do it properly or safely in such a confined space, they had no idea, but they would cross that bridge when they came to it.

"One, two, three... lift!" instructed Fleet, and with him at the back and Sally at the front, they managed to hoist Bertha up the stairs, into the ringing room and onto the bed as if they had been doing this whole paramedic lark for years!

"Her breathing's getting shallower," observed Bev anxiously, "and I'm barely detecting a pulse at all." Hazel was tempted to wonder if a lack of warm blood flowing in her veins might just be the normal state of affairs for Bertha, but thought better of voicing this idea. They had to try and save her, even if it meant that she would probably give their Health and Safety inspection a fail on coming round from her coma.

"Unplug the Dimplex," said Hazel to Veronica, who was mopping Derek's brow as he started to come round. "We need to get this ventilator up and running. Oh, and put the defibrillator on charge while you're at it, just in case."

Instantly, the ventilator came to life, beeping and flashing an array of little LEDs and digital numbers. Muriel could remember how these things worked. (She had sat by her husband's side for a week in the Princess Royal hospital in Telford after he nearly choked to death when one of her Wensleydale Unmentionables had gone down the wrong way.)

"Put that on there, insert that, press that button and that should do it," she told Hazel. And - hey presto! - it worked! The colour came back to Bertha's cheeks and the machine was clearly making her chest rise and fall at a steady and satisfying rate. The heart monitor showed a regular heartbeat and her pulse appeared to be relatively normal, or so said Muriel in rather more technical terms, using words like 'systolic' and 'stenosis'. (Veronica suspected she was just quoting bits of dialogue memorised from watching back-to-back *Casualty* on UK Gold whilst gorging on Terry's Chocolate Oranges.)

"Excellent!" said Hazel, once it was clear that the machinery was all functioning as intended and Bertha's condition was critical but stable. "Job well done! Time to put the kettle on, I think."

"I'll do the honours," offered Veronica. "The pot's still up at the village hall, though, I think. I know it's uncouth, but I assume that, under the circumstances, nobody will mind if I drop one in your cup and leave you to sort out your own teabagging? Derek - a nice milky one for you...?"

"Ooh, that's a cracking cup of Tetley!" said Fleet, breaking the silence as they all sat round the ringing room benches a short while later, steaming mugs in hand. Phyllis looked sorry for herself with her bandaged arm, but did her best to put a brave face on it. Dympna, meanwhile, was much perked up thanks to a change of underwear and a thorough restructuring of her support girdle set-up in the vestry toilet. Mike stared ahead in stunned silence, still reeling from the shock of her telling him every graphic detail of the back-end collapse.

Derek sat with a quite unnecessary blanket around his shoulders, the result of Muriel having fallen prey to another one of her half-remembered St John's Ambulance routines that had merged into something from a *Holby City* air disaster scene. He was pretty much back to normal, and, if anything, needed fewer layers on, not more, what with the stuffy air of the fully-populated ringing room and his tight SACY uniform still neatly in place.

Bertha whirred and hissed mechanically in the corner on the ventilator, which was doing a grand job of keeping her alive. Whilst she was safely unconscious,

Hazel snuck a peek at the clipboard to see how the inspection had gone. *Bugger!* It wasn't good news. Even if they hadn't virtually killed her, they were still headed for an 'Inadequate' rating. The thought did cross her mind that pulling the plug - totally accidentally, of course - would provide a quick and tidy solution, but she couldn't really entertain such a horrible idea for more than a second's worth of wishful thinking. And before she could even move on to thinking through the better solution - namely, how to make proper amends and earn a 'Satisfactory' - Crispin, Dom and Hastings came clattering their way back through from the vestry door, utterly drenched from head to foot.

"We're trapped!" cried Crispin. "Totally cut off! The river's burst its banks and turned us into an island!"

"And worse than that," continued Dom, "the old oak's fallen right across Church Lane, taking the phone lines with it. So, even if we could get through to the village, we won't be able to call anyone. And there's no way an ambulance is getting through any time soon. There are more trees about to come down too, so who knows how many other roads are going to be blocked!"

"It's too dangerous to try and come through the main church door," continued Crispin, standing back while Hastings shook himself off vigorously in the side aisle. "Too many branches and bits of masonry coming down. That's why we came in the vicar's private entrance. It's the only available access, but it's a hell of a tight squeeze. We'll barely get the stretcher over the threshold, let alone round the angle."

"We're going to have to stay put for now and manage by ourselves," said Dom with a doubtful tone in his voice.

"Well, with trained St John's Ambulance members and all of this state-of-the-art medical technology at our disposal," replied Fleet, "we should be able to ride it out."

"Yes," agreed Bev. "What can possibly go wrong?"

And, as if by magic, that which could possibly go wrong did just that: first a blinding light that flooded the church through every one of its windows, followed by a deafening crash that was so close and earth-shattering that it could only have been the enormous yew that overhung the lych gate. With the fall of the tree, the power was instantly cut and the whole church was plunged into a state of absolute darkness, in which nobody dared say anything or move.

The first to utter any sound at all was Hastings, who whimpered pathetically, voicing what everybody else was feeling inside. Then, worse still: the machine stopped bleeping, the ventilator gave out one last breath and Bertha fell into a deathly silence.

"Oh Lord, whatever do we do now?" asked Sally helplessly. "Has anybody got a torch at least?"

"There are some big candles in the vestry, for when the vicar's in one of his High Church moods," suggested Muriel. She called down to Crispin and Dom to tell them where to look. "Second drawer down in the corner chest. Not the armoire!" (The armoire was where the vicar kept his freshly laundered vestments, and she didn't want them fumbling around in the dark and inadvertently fingering his pristine cincture.)

"Found them!" shouted Dom eventually, and before long, they were out in the main body of the church holding forth the miraculous gift of light. They worked their way up into the ringing room where everyone was waiting anxiously for their arrival. Veronica and Muriel were already removing Bertha's mouthpiece to prepare her for CPR, and now that they had at least a glimmer of light with which to find their way, they would be able to get started before her lips turned completely blue.

"I'll compress the chest while you do the mouth-to-mouth, Muriel," said Veronica, bagsying the less stomach-churning of the two tasks. "What's the rhythm again? 'Nellie the Elephant', isn't it?"

"No," said Muriel. "Research has shown that to be a bit too lively. I hear that 'Shine Jesus Shine' is recommended now."

And so, off went Veronica, bouncing away with gusto on Bertha's sternum. "Join in, everybody! It'll help me keep the rhythm going!"

Dom winced involuntarily at this unexpected outing for his absolute least favourite hymn. Even 'Colours of Day' or 'One More Step Along the World I Go' would have been preferable. He felt like mentioning that 'Staying Alive' by the Bee Gees would do the job just as effectively, but kept his mouth shut, reasoning that Veronica was probably too old to know it and that teaching it to her now was not really a priority.

They sang as joyfully as they could manage under the circumstances, trying their best to keep to the general mood of 'Shine Jesus Shine'. Veronica paused for Muriel to administer the requisite two breaths during the "Shine on me, shine on me" bit before launching back into her vigorous pumping to the rousing chorus, which actually sounded rather lovely thanks to Phyllis' warbly soprano and Fleet's rich baritone holding it all together.

"How's she doing?" asked Sally when they got to the end of the hymn. "Do we need to go around again?"

"Looks like it," said Muriel, her lipstick now

smudged halfway across her cheek. "Does anyone else want a go?"

"We should probably stick to social distancing rules as closely as we can," stammered Bev. "And you certainly seem to know what you're doing, Muriel."

"I'll do the compressions, though!" volunteered Hazel with unexpected enthusiasm. "I've got the idea now and that will give you a rest, Veronica."

"Well, just quickly before you start up again, loosen that bra. It's cutting into her like a cheese wire!" said Veronica, shaking her head in disbelief after a quick glance at the label. Her forty years' experience in charge of Worcester's British Home Stores lingerie department had made her one of the region's foremost experts on bra size. "Whoever told her she was a 30B wants shooting. I can tell just by looking that she's a 34DD."

Hazel did the honours, secretly wondering how long it had been since she last undid a bra other than her own. Then, off they went again for a second time, and now that everyone had got the catchy tune and lyrics back into their heads properly, it really was sounding way up there with anything that the full Frotting choir could manage. Phyllis even considered asking Dom and Crispin to nip down to get the organ up and running if they were going to be in it for the long haul, but it really didn't seem necessary, such was the quality of their unaccompanied rendition. Would it work in a power cut, though? Phyllis wondered. Well, even if not, surely Crispin could help Dom out by doing a bit of manual pumping and at least get something out of it.

Out of nowhere, another violent flash of magnesium white burst through the windows, along with a horsewhip thundercrack which broke everyone's train of thought. It was louder than any of those that had gone before, and closer than ever. The storm must now have been directly overhead, reaching its jagged claws down, down, seeking out a helpless point of contact. A victim.

Oh, Bob! thought Sally. *You would know how to get us out of this mess. Where are you when we need you?*

And then, from out of the darkness above them, came a voice, a voice that could have been The Good Lord himself...

"It looks like you could all use a bit of a hand down there. Can I be of assistance?"

Bob!

Sally stared upwards, frozen in disbelief, as he climbed down the ladder from the bell chamber, sporting a helicopter-rescue jumpsuit in a fetching shade of khaki, along with a huge shiny helmet. Was she dreaming? This was the last thing she was expecting. *Bob! Here and now, at this very moment!* It was such a shock that she could barely think what to do. Part of her was so scared that she instinctively wanted to run out, out, away to safety. Another part of her said she should hold firm and make it… make what? Make it seem that none of this was happening, that it was all just some impossible dream. But the greatest part of her screamed: "RUN IN! RUN IN! RUN INTO HIS LOVING ARMS, AND MAKE SURE HE NEVER LETS GO!"

So this is what she did.

The warmth of his embrace made time stand still. It was as if he had never been away, as if he had always been right there with her, every minute of every hour of every day. Which he had been, of course, there, in the deepest recesses of her heart.

"My darling, Sally," he whispered to her huskily.

"Oh, how I have missed you! More than you will ever know!"

"No more than I have missed you, my dear, sweet Bob!" she replied, staring deep into his sapphire eyes. "Promise you'll never leave me again!"

"I promise, Sally, I promise," he declared with such seriousness that she believed him to the very core of her being. "From now on, wherever I go, I will take you with me. The National 12-Bell, the Church Stretton District AGM, the FODS dinner…"

Crispin, eavesdropping as usual, perked up at this, only to be immediately let down as Robert continued…

"…of which I'm not an active member, you understand, just an associate well-wisher. I've only been to it with my good friend Richard occasionally, just for the craic…"

"Wherever you want to take me," said Sally, "I promise I'll always come with you. Even to the Church Stretton District AGM. I'd go through any torture just to be by your side. Just you try and stop me!" And she laughed through her tears of joy and relief, allowing the maelstrom of emotions to whirl and pulse through her every nerve and vein. "But first, as you can see, we've got a bit of a problem…"

Much as they had been keen to pause and bear witness to the happy reunion of Bob and Sally, the other ringers had done their civic duty and continued gamely in their attempts to keep Bertha on the right side of death's door. 'Shine Jesus Shine' was now into its sixteenth go-around and still there were few, if any, signs of improvement.

"Good evening, everybody," said Robert to the congregation gathered around the prostrate body of Bertha. "The Ringing Reservists have winched me down to assess the situation here, but it's so precarious outside that we aren't able to land the chopper. I see that we have a casualty. Was she caught in the floods?"

"No," replied Hazel. "It's a long story. But basically, we've lost all power, so the ventilator's gone down and we've had to keep her going with CPR. I don't know how much longer we can carry on…"

"Oh, do help us, Bob!" interrupted Veronica, feeling the need for an injection of added drama.

"I think we might be dealing with supraventricular tachycardia," added Muriel, throwing in another little nugget that she'd picked up from *Casualty*, "and a possible subarachnoid haemorrhage. If only we had an IV line, we could infiltrate a dilute solution of epinephrine and/or adrenaline… Or even 2% lidocaine would do!"

"You're just making it up now, Muriel," said Veronica, rolling her eyes. "Let the man come to his own conclusions."

"In my opinion," said Robert, having briefly assessed the lie of the land, "the best thing we can do is get the power back on. Have you not engaged the dynamos yet?"

"Dynamos?" asked Mike, getting suddenly excited by the mention of something in the general ballpark of machinery.

"Did I not tell you?" replied Robert. "Oh, silly me! I completely forgot to mention it! Just before I headed off around the world to ring peals in Richard Branson's Mile-High Virgin BellJet, I secretly popped up into the bell chamber and hooked your bell wheels up to a full set of experimental dynamos that I'd knocked up over a spare evening here and there in my garage. I thought we might as well start to harness some of our otherwise wasted energy and sell any excess back to the National Grid. Green Deal and all that. Just a couple of peals should be enough to power the whole village for a week!"

"I hope you remembered to get a faculty," said Derek with an ominous wag of the finger.

"Oh, you don't need to worry about that," replied

Bob. "The bishop plays golf with the Junior Minister for Climate Change. You can do what you like to your church on the energy-saving front nowadays. Solar panels, composting toilets, graveyard worm farms… As long as it's green, it gets the green light!"

"God, I've missed his puns," thought Sally, staring at her Bob with an all-consuming passion. *"He's so clever!"*

"So, all we need to do is engage this lever…" Bob showed everyone where it was located over in the corner where two defunct Ewbanks, a lightly charred Electrolux and a Dyson with a cracked ball languished for all eternity, now that Henry had usurped them "…and then just get ringing. The dynamos will kick in straight away and - hey presto! - power will be restored."

"So, what are we waiting for?" urged Sally, keen to put the system to the test. "Come on, everyone, grab hold!"

Almost as soon as they began to ring up, the lights started to flicker, as if creating visual echoes of the lightning flashes that continued to intensify outside. The sound of the bells beginning to chime gradually filled the space, covering the white noise of the rain which battered against the leaded windows like catapulted scoops of gravel. Within thirty seconds, as the momentum in the bells really started to get the wheels moving, the lights were on fully, bathing the ringing room in a calming, mellow glow.

And then, from Bertha, a bleep!

"Oh, thank the Lord!" exclaimed Muriel, who was waiting on tenterhooks with Phyllis, Dympna, Veronica and Derek around the motionless body. "She's breathing again, and we've got a pulse!"

"Thank the Lord, indeed!" agreed Hazel, who was on the Treble and nearly had it up already.

"Moving in His ever-mysterious ways," said Bev, who was ringing next to her on the Two. "That he should inspire our Bob to come up with his little initiative, and that it should immediately turn out to be life- as well as energy-saving… incredible!"

"Bravo, Bob!" boomed Fleet, who had grabbed hold next to Bev on the third. "That's just the kind of initiative-taking that we like to see in the world of bathroom sales. Take note, young Crispin, take note!"

Crispin, who had eagerly taken up the rear, not only for the perennial joy of bonging behind, but also so as to keep his distance from the ever-irritating Fleet, nodded and smiled wanly from his position over on the tenor rope. God, his boss could be a pompous pain in the arse at times. In fact, not just at times, but all the time. If only the object of his affections knew what she was letting herself in for. The idea of Beverley and Sir Fleet spliced together in holy matrimony? One thing's for sure, Crispin would not be playing the organ for that wedding for any money. On the positive side, though, at least it might give the man something else to focus on apart from flushing mechanisms and the latest advances in grout technology…

Next to Crispin was Dom, with his reassuring presence and steady guiding hand. "I'll talk you through it if you have to turn it in at any point," he whispered to Crispin, who shuddered at the prospect with an almost visible frisson of rapture. "Just don't let it drop and keep it moving. That way, you'll be fine, even if Robert wants us all to tackle his Double

Norwich."

Completing the band were Mike on the Six, Robert on the Five and Sally on the Four. Derek had magnanimously and sensibly volunteered to sit out after his little episode, and used it as an opportunity to deal with that pile of ropes that needed some urgent maintenance. (Hazel had had to put whipping further down her list of priorities, what with all of the tightening and lubrication that she had been needing to undertake upstairs over the summer, so Derek had volunteered to do the honours on her behalf.) And so, with waxed thread in hand, he got busy and drifted off into a mindful state, fully absorbed into the slowing rhythm of the nearly-raised bells. Veronica and Muriel, meanwhile, were delighted to hold onto the mantle of carers for the sick and injured, monitoring Bertha's machinery whilst doling out painkillers to Phyllis for her still-throbbing arm and extra pads to Dympna to help her keep control of the ongoing developments below.

"I've not felt anything quite like it since Crispin popped out!" she announced on her way back off down to the lavatory with a fresh bundle. "Even then, the obstetrician said I might as well cut my losses and have it all out, but you never know whether you're going to want another one at some point. But I shouldn't grumble really. It's nothing compared to what my sister went through having those big bouncing twins…"

Thankfully, Dympna was already out of the door before she could elaborate any further, which gave everyone else time to steel their nerves and, more importantly, their stomachs in readiness for the inevitable continuation of the story on her return.

"Stand!" called Robert when he could see that everyone was well and truly up and, without a hitch, the ringers stood their bells and awaited further instruction. Almost immediately, with the dynamos no longer moving, the lights began to fade ever so slightly, and it was clear that they would need to get ringing again pretty damn sharpish if they didn't want Bertha to slip back into cardiac arrest.

"A short touch of Bristol," suggested Robert, "for old time's sake?"

"I'm game," nodded Sally with a twinkle in her eye.

"You call it," he suggested. "Let's see how you've come on during my absence."

"The pleasure will be all mine."

And so, off they went, enjoying the challenge of some serious ringing for a change, and all in the name of critical life support. Once everyone was fully settled into the rhythm, Robert switched to ringing one-handed, a little trick that he had picked up a few years back on the Sandbach course.

Is there nothing this man can't do? thought Sally.

Bloody show-off… thought Mike.

Is he drunk or something? thought Bev.

Erm… Health and Safety? thought Hazel.

Robert's dextrous little manoeuvre enabled him to whip out his walkie-talkie and talk through the evacuation plan.

"Foxtrot Uniform, come in! What's the situation outside? Over."

A crackled response came straight through. The news wasn't good.

"Water's still rising, Victor Romeo, and the wind is nearing hurricane force. We have to find a safe place to land as a matter of urgency. You're on your own until the storm passes, I'm afraid. Can you manage? Over."

"Roger, Foxtrot Uniform. We have a casualty on life-support, we're running her on bell power, and I have a band of very competent Surprise Major ringers. We'll be just fine. We will ring for as long as it takes. See you on the other side. Over and out."

Robert paused momentarily to let the full magnitude of his words fully sink in. Everyone gave each other nervous glances, but it was clear that they would all rise to the challenge. He could sense it. They were bell ringers, for God's sake. Sturdy English bell ringers, made from the strongest of spirits, the truest of grits, the saltiest of spunks. They wouldn't let a once-in-a-millennium weather event get in their way, just as they didn't let a global pandemic stop them. No, they came out for Queen and country, every week without fail, to stake their rightful claim to the full fifteen minutes on alternate ropes... as long as nobody had touched them during the previous 72 hours, in which case they thought they'd better leave it, just to be on the safe side. (They were warriors, yes, but they were sensible warriors, not hell-bent kamikaze risk-takers!)

"It's going to be a long night," said Robert, putting away the walkie-talkie to focus fully on the end of Sally's Bristol. They brought it round perfectly and Sally called out a triumphant *"This is all!"* to the collective satisfaction of all involved.

"Good work, everyone," called Robert over the crisp and rapid rounds. "Any suggestions for what else we should ring?"

"Well, I'm dying to have a crack at your Velvet Willy for starters," said Crispin daringly.

"Oh, you know about that, do you?" asked an intrigued Robert.

"We've been getting ourselves nicely polished for you," said Sally, blushing. "All of those new methods we came up with back at Girthsmount Hill, we can ring every one of them now. Well, in theory, at least. I hope you don't mind."

"Mind?" exclaimed Robert. "Why ever would I mind? Nothing would give me more pleasure than to run through the whole gamut. What better opportunity could there be? And can I take it that everyone's had a good look at York Hunt?"

"Of course," replied Sally. "They're all totally clued up on that. Even Crispin's got stuck in."

Crispin gave a cheery thumbs-up, and the others nodded eagerly to confirm that Sally had very definitely put them in the picture.

"So we can all have a good stab at your Frotting Alliance," she continued, impressing Bob with her confidence and her no-nonsense approach to running a practice. "After that, we can go straight into my Fanybong and then how about we all try to get our first blows in my Frotting Surprise?"

"Frotting Surprise?" asked Robert. "You kept that

one up your sleeve!"

"Well, if I didn't, then it wouldn't be a surprise now, would it?"

She's getting as sharp as me with the puns, thought Robert with an inner smirk. *I'm going to have to up my game!*

"Right then," said Sally. "We've at least got something to keep us busy for a good while. By the sound of that rain outside, things are only going to get worse…"

An hour and a half later, they had covered an impressive repertoire of methods old and new. The Velvet Willy had gone down a treat and, whilst there had been a bit of looseness round the back in the Fanybong, Dom had talked Crispin out of it and they held it together to avoid a messy fire-out. Ultimately, though, everyone found their feet beautifully and the whole experience was relaxed enough for Sally and Robert to make up for lost time in whispered tones.

"How come you're back so soon, then?" she asked him. "It's only a week or so since I watched you all fly out on the Six O'Clock News. You should be in India now, shouldn't you? Or thereabouts?"

"No, it all went a bit pear-shaped, if the truth be told," confessed Robert. "The CCCCCCR risk assessment covered every conceivable base bar one: namely, the possibility that the Queen might get tinnitus. She was fine on the Amsterdam leg. Really enjoying it, in fact, tapping her feet to the rhythm of our Reverse Margaret Marsh. But by the time we disembarked in Abu Dhabi, she was clearly the worse for wear, unable to shake off the incessant ringing in her ears. *'I'd rather take Ryanair than get back on that bloody Virgin BellJet!'* were her exact words, and so that was the end of that. Platinum Jubilee tour cancelled and the plane flown straight back for scrappage. Such a shame!"

"And what about Tess Stringer?" asked Sally. "Was she able to keep her hands off you?" Sally knew she was sounding petulant, and that jealousy was such an ugly emotion, but she didn't care. She had to know that Robert had remained true to his promises.

"Tess?!" scoffed Robert. "Don't you worry about Tess. We won't be seeing anything more of her for a very long time."

"Oh really? How come?"

"Well, as soon as we landed at Abu Dhabi, she stood her bell at backstroke and stormed off. Lee Drong had corrected one of her calls and, my word, you've never seen someone fly off the handle quite like it. Such a temper! Called us all a bunch of hopeless amateurs and said they were shit bells anyway."

"Attention-seeking as always…" tutted Sally, rolling her eyes.

"Bells on planes aren't challenging enough for her, apparently. So the upshot of it is that she's now hooked up with Elon Musk and is project-managing some silly First-Bells-In-Space idea of his. They're putting them on board his Amphibious Roving Space Explorer and heading off with the Kardashians to ring where no man has rung before: amid the red rocks of Mars, beneath the liquid methane seas of Titan, upon the frozen ball of Charon... A case of one-upmanship if ever there was one, but at least she'll be out of the way, floating somewhere beyond the dark side of Uranus for the next twenty years."

"And what about the gravity issue?" asked a bemused Sally.

"Elon's bells will be so good that they won't need gravity, or so says Tess. But let her find out the hard way. She'll have trouble storming out when they're all stuck out there in the middle of the Kuiper Belt, won't she?"

"So, we're actually rid of her?" asked Sally, barely able to conceal her joy.

"Well and truly," nodded Robert. "Nothing and no one can come between us ever again. Of that you have my word."

"Oh Bob!" said Sally, a tear of relief welling up in her eye. Then she paused for a moment, gripped by a sudden flash of inspiration. "The Virgin BellJet…"

"Yes, Sally?"

"They're not going to scrap the bells too, are they? Tell me it's just the plane."

"It's all got to go, I'm afraid. Damaged goods. Who's going to want them now they've left the Queen with irreversible tinnitus?"

"Me, Bob!" said Sally urgently. "I want them! Or rather, we want them, here, for Frotting! We've already got all of the funding together. It would be such a shame if they just got melted back down."

"Leave it with me," whispered Bob reassuringly. "I'll see what I can do…"

"Take me off!" shouted Mike out of nowhere. "Take me off, Sally, quickly!"

"Of course!" she stammered. "So sorry! I quite forgot where we were for a moment there."

"Sorry…" Robert mouthed at her for contributing to the moment of distraction, but they quickly slotted back into their respective places in Mike's Slack Bottom and readied themselves for the imminent switchover to Hazel's Twatt.

"My word, can it get any worse out there?" wondered Fleet aloud, as the sound of the trees yawning in the gale carried through into the church.

"I dread to think. How's Bertha?" Hazel asked the ladies, who were still gathered around her bed, monitoring the situation.

"Stable," replied Veronica. "Probably a good time to put the kettle on again. Any takers?" Enthusiastic agreement came from all quarters and so Veronica headed downstairs to do the honours once more.

"There might be a few of my prune granola nuggets down there in a Tupperware, left over from Teatime Church if you have a rummage," Muriel called after her.

"Can't wait…" whispered Dominic snidely to Crispin, who responded with a cheeky giggle. They had been getting to know each other better than ever before over the course of the evening's ringing, and, to Crispin's joy, Dom finally took the bait and invited him over to Granser next Sunday afternoon for a full organ tour. (*"If you do come over, you can help me with a bit of maintenance work. Make sure you put your boiler suit on, oh, and bring some knee pads,"* Dom had told him. *"I think I might need a new blower, so there could be quite a bit of kneeling required."*) Crispin was already buzzing at the prospect and thought that this could be the start of something big. Or at least it would be if they managed to get through this wretched storm in one piece…

Torrents were raging by now against the walls of the

church, making the tower shake more than the bells had ever done. Distant sirens could just be made out above the roaring of the water and the lashing of the rain. Lightning flashes continued to punctuate the air, illuminating the body of the church, which appeared to tremble in terror of what was soon inevitably to come.

It was just as Hazel opened her mouth to announce *"Go, Twatt Bob Major!"* that a thunderous crash shook the whole building and all hell broke loose. The floodwaters, which had until now only been trickling in slowly beneath the tight seal of the church's ancient oak door, finally broke through. The door was blasted off its hinges and flung across the floor towards the font, and everyone stared in horror from the ringing room as a tsunami of churning, chocolate-brown water smashed through into the body of the church. In a split second, it had filled the space and its sheer volume and power had lifted the pews, which span and bobbed around on the surface like broken matches.

Suddenly, from below, someone let out a horrific scream of terror, like a snared hyena. Hastings, who had been hiding with Henry in fear of the storm, growled and barked an urgent response.

"Veronica!" gasped Phyllis, as she spotted a writhing mass of floral mauve come gushing out of the kitchen and into the west transept, thrashing its arms about like an octopus on crystal meth. "Grab hold of the rood screen!"

Veronica had always been rather circumspect about the rood screen, what with all of its somewhat too erotic instructional medieval carvings of cavorting naked sinners being poked by demons with forks. For fear of seeming excessively prudish, though, she chose not to voice these particular reservations at PCC meetings, arguing rather that it should be removed, along with most of the pews, to create better sightlines and make way for comfier (i.e. more haemorrhoid-friendly) chairs. Now, however, in a delicious irony that was not lost upon Phyllis and Muriel, who watched her plight on tenterhooks from the ringing mezzanine, Veronica could thank the Devil's own oaken phallus for her salvation, as she grabbed it in the nick of time to prevent her otherwise inevitable drowning.

"Hold on tight, Vee," called Derek, who had conveniently just finished his last bit of whipping, "and I'll get one of these ropes to you in a jiffy!"

However, the water kept on rising inexorably, and Veronica was forced to use the rood screen as a sort of makeshift ladder, rising up on the surface past diabolical wooden orgies, in a Dantean ascent from the lowest circles of Hell. Within seconds, water was up to the level of the horrified ringers, cascading over the balcony and washing around their feet.

"If only we still had the emergency slide," wailed Phyllis, "then we could all use it as a life raft!" As if on cue, it floated down the nave and swirled around, fully deflated and no longer fit for purpose, like a used banana-flavoured novelty condom for a sperm whale.

"Don't jump on it, Veronica!" instructed Derek, who could see that she was considering it. "It's not safe! Wait until we can get a rope to you!" Veronica nodded feebly that she understood and clung on as tightly as she could to a naked wooden fornicator being mercilessly boiled in tar.

"Oh no!" sobbed Sally, who had a clear view from the Four of the drama unfolding on the rood screen. "Veronica won't be able to hold on much longer! What can we do?!"

"Don't stop ringing!" shouted Robert. "If the lights stay on, we can still be seen from outside. It's our only hope!"

Sobs of fear punctuated the sound of the vicious, freezing waters, which had quickly reached knee-height. But another more ominous sound then focused everyone's minds: the slowing bleep of Bertha.

"The ventilator!" shrieked Muriel. It was sparking

and hissing as it stood there in nearly two feet of water, clearly already beyond rescue or repair. As it slowly gave up the ghost, Muriel called out the digits on the heartbeat monitor: "54 beats per minute… 37… 21… Oh, please, no! Look! 13…"

"Just keep ringing!" Robert instructed the band. "We must keep ringing for as long as we possibly can! We must never give up!"

"6!" wailed Muriel. "Look! 2…! She's going…! She's gone…!"

The bleeps became a single fading note, which then, with a final blue flash and a hideous crackle, slipped away to nothingness. One by one, the lights followed suit. The candles that Dom and Crispin had brought back from the vestry had already long since been washed away. The waxen length of one of them bobbed past Sally's leg, like a bone gnawed free of its flesh, just perceptible in the glow from the final pitiful bulb, which flickered… which flickered… which flickered… and died.

"She's coming round!"

"Oh, thank Heavens!"

"I thought we'd lost her for a minute there."

"Quick, somebody grab that blanket and get some sugary tea."

These were the first words that she heard on waking. The voices that made them were somehow distorted, distant, barely human. Her face felt wet, but why was the wetness moving?

"Hastings!" shrilled another voice. "Get back and leave her be! She's been through enough without your contribution!"

"The water!" Sally gasped as she tried to open her eyes. "Has the water gone?"

"What water, my darling?" whispered Robert, as he leant over. She stared up into his crystalline eyes, and saw, around his head, a halo of bell ropes reaching up into the heavens.

"She must need a drink," suggested Bev. "Let her sip from this bottle."

Robert tilted Sally's head up gently and let the soothing drops moisten her parched lips.

"Bertha!" gasped Sally suddenly, her eyes widening in horror at the memories that were bombarding her waking brain. "Where's Bertha?"

"Don't worry. Just relax. She's not coming until next week," said Hazel. "The risk assessments are all done and I've even remembered to chuck out the out-of-date Quality Street. It will all be fine!"

"But... but..." stammered Sally, trying to lever herself up to look round the ringing room. "She was here! We killed her!"

"Oh dear," muttered Veronica to Muriel. "She's clearly delusional. You didn't accidentally put magic mushrooms in those vol-au-vents again, did you?"

"Don't be silly!" replied Muriel with a frown. "It's just your classic confusion following an episode of vasovagal syncope..."

"Vasovagal Syncope? I've not seen that!" said Phyllis. "Is it anything like Midsomer Murders? What channel's it on?"

"Fainting, she means," explained Veronica. "Sally's just had a bit of a faint. Pushing herself that bit too far. I did say that this whole idea might be a bit too ambitious, but you can't stop her once she puts her mind to something. She's like a dog with a bone..."

"I don't understand..." said Sally weakly, as the ringers gathered around to welcome her back into reality. They were all there: Crispin, Dom, Fleet, Bev, Mike, Hazel and, of course, her very own Bob. The ladies and Derek milled around too, clearing empty bottles and plates, and putting away what looked like little foldaway tables borrowed from the village hall. Martin Draycott and Brian Farnett were there too; Sally could see them out of the corner of her eye polishing off a plate of Muriel's ubiquitous Wensleydale Unmentionables. The atmosphere seemed oddly joyous, although the joy seemed tinged with relief as if they had all achieved some wonderful success that was not entirely expected.

"There was a flood..." continued Sally, trying to piece it all back together. "You had been away to rescue the Lundy martyrs… No, that's not right… That was just a cover story… No, you went on the big plane with the bells… And then you came back to save us all!"

"Did anyone remember to make that sugary tea?" asked Mike. "She's clearly still not all there yet. A plane with bells?! Nice idea, but still…"

"And now Tess Stringer's gone off with Elon Musk and the Kardashians to ring beneath the frozen seas of Titan… That is true, isn't it, Robert?" begged Sally with urgency. "That wasn't a lie, was it, just to make me feel better? She has really gone off in the Amphibious Roving Space Explorer, hasn't she, Tess Stringer?"

"Calm down, dear," said Robert quietly and without even the first hint of a patronising tone. "You're still in a state of deep confusion. There is no Tess Stringer. There are no plane bells or space bells or anything like that. And the Kardashians certainly don't spend their spare time ringing. I doubt they've got any suitable clothes and just imagine the havoc it would play with their nail varnish!"

"But… but…" stuttered Sally in disbelief, "everybody's ringing nowadays, aren't they? It's taken the world by storm. The Eurovision Bong Contest and all that. Don't you remember?"

"You've clearly just had a very, very weird trip to La-La Land," explained Robert reassuringly. "You were even muttering incoherently at one point about Ant and Dec hosting the ART Awards."

"Gosh, I've no idea where that came from... Am I going mad?" asked Sally, unsure if she wanted to hear an answer to that. Robert just held her hand and gave it a squeeze of reassurance. *'No, you aren't going mad'*, it told her. *'You are now back in the room'*. "So, there aren't hordes of A-list celebrities bringing ringing to the fame-crazed masses?"

"No, my darling," said Robert. "Ringing is as geeky and unfashionable as it's always been. Beyoncé has been getting into Morris dancing, admittedly, but I really can't see the appropriation of traditional English culture going any further than that."

"You've got to hand it to Beyoncé, though," chipped in Dom. "She is bloody good with a pair of hankies."

"So..." asked Sally, pausing as a new old normal slotted itself into place in her waking brain, "if none of what I thought happened just happened... then what *did* happen?"

Robert lent closer to tell her ever so quietly, and everyone else fell silent so as to hear her reaction.

"Remember those new bells you were hankering

after?"

"Yes!" said Sally. "I remember!"

"Well, my darling," he continued. "You just rang them for the very first time…"

"Oh, Bob! Can it be true?!" Sally was overcome with emotion. Rapture seized her every fibre. Ecstatic tears sprang from her eyes. "What did I ring?"

Bob paused. She fixed his gaze. Her prince was here, and he stooped to rouse her once and for all from her infinite-seeming sleep. His kiss was warm. It was lingering. It was magical… And it worked!

"I remember, Bob! Oh, I remember everything!" The whole exquisite memory was suddenly there again, sparkling and alive in her now vibrant mind...

"My first long length!"

Hereford Diocesan Guild

Frotting St James, St James the Dismembered
Saturday, 3 September 2022 in 6h 11 (12–3–4 in E)
10080 Spliced Surprise Major (12 methods)

840 each of Frotting Alliance, Brown Willy, Tittybong,
Fanybedwell, Cuntastorp, Velvet Bottom, Onacock, Twatt,
Cocking Alliance, Velvet Willy, Fanybong & Frotting
Surprise

Composed by Mike Lapper, Sally B Tuggin & Major
Robert Liddell

1	Hazel O Fluck
2	Beverley Belleau
3	Fleet Carr
4	Sally B Tuggin
5	Maj. Robert Liddell
6	Mike Lapper (C)
7	Dominic Topp
8	Crispin D P Hipkiss

Umpires: Derek Beavis, Martin Draycott, Brian Farnett

*First performance on the new Meltham, Downe & Bymore bells.
First splicing of all 12 methods in Mike Lapper's Battered
Sausage project.
First long length: 4 & 8*

I recovered quickly, in case you were wondering. I had only been out for five minutes, ten at the most, so they told me, and that whole strange hallucination - the flood and everything that led up to it - was soon but a distant blip. On reflection, of course, I realised that the flood was just my unconscious mind telling me that I needed a seriously big wee and to wake up before the dam burst. Once that problem was solved, much to my relief, everything started to feel better. My shoulders ached for a week or two afterwards, admittedly, and those six hours of non-stop standing did make me a little sluggish when it came to moving around. But it was worth it, every minute of it! Not only was it my first long length (and Crispin's, bless him!), but it was the first performance on the new bells, the bells I had dreamed of for as long as I could remember.

They are superb, the envy of the nation, some even saying that they are the finest ring of eight ever cast! Better than their gorgeous resonance, better than their perfect equilibrium, better than their heavenly music, better than all of these, though, is the magic that they have worked on all who ring them.

Muriel, for example, has found a strength and determination to progress that none of us would ever have imagined. She has trodden the Brown Pathway to its farthest possible reaches and, yes, she can now ring up any of the front six without the slightest fuss or difficulty. In fact, she was so thrilled when she managed to get the Six up for the first time, that she then regaled us all with her latest culinary creation: wholegrain Dijon custard slices. (A work in progress, admittedly, but like the ringing, the cookery is heading in the right direction.)

Veronica, likewise, has made a real quantum leap. Her Reverse Canterbury Pleasure Place is now a thing of genuine beauty: neat and crisp on the way up and the way down, not a blow out of place. Derek has told her that learning to Treble Dodge is next on the list, and she has promised to throw herself into it as soon as she's given her new ringing bra a bit of time to bed in.

Having witnessed Veronica's triumph, Phyllis took the bull by the horns and she too is now looking at Reverse Canterbury with a serious eye, alongside her first proper touches of Grandsire. She has also personally spearheaded the rationalisation of the Quality Street situation and has divided them into separate 'MAY CONTAIN NUTS' and 'UNLIKELY TO CONTAIN NUTS, BUT ON YOUR OWN HEAD BE IT' boxes.

Derek is like a pig in muck with the new bells, it has to be said. If the truth be told, he was starting to struggle with the old ones, what with his weakening arthritic grip and markedly increasing stoop. Now, however, the ease of turning them in has put him back on track with his Surprise Minor, and he is raring to go for his residential week down in Kent with the Society of Ancient College Youths. He's already sorted out his composition - Dickford Water, so he tells me - and is secretly confident that it will cause a bit of a splash. (I did try to drop him a subtle hint that, somewhere at the back of my mind, I had an inkling that Dickford Water might not be advisable, and shouldn't he maybe just stick to Cambridge? But who am I to pour cold water on his admirable ambitions?)

Hazel is similarly in her element what with all that brand new gubbins up in the bell chamber to check up on. Although, in all honesty, Meltham, Downe & Bymore have done such a fantastic job - brand-new stainless-steel frame, self-aligning bearings, state-of-the-art clappers with self-lubricating nylon bushes - that there's really precious little that she can tinker with up there. So she has made it her mission for the time being to support towers in need of technical advice. First on the list? The Vernet Lesbians, of course, who have reported some problems with misaligned garter holes and consequent abrasion to a number of their flanges. Oh, and one or two of their dinglers have worked themselves loose. With Hastings wormed, chipped and passported up in readiness, Hazel will be packing her best heavy-duty spanner set and grease gun in the VW camper van, and off to the Pyrenees the pair of them will go this Saturday.

Both Hazel and Derek have added cause for celebration, incidentally, after the long-dreaded inspection visit from Bertha Gorse turned out to be mercilessly brief and virtually painless. By a pure stroke of luck, she had decided to kill two birds with one stone and started the evening by dropping in unannounced at Granser-on-Severn. There, she discovered breaches of Health and Safety good practice that would turn your hair whiter than Mrs Cattiton's. Namely, an elderly Hoover SuctionQueen 4000 whose cable had been chewed by rodents; bat droppings on the bookshelves; frayed, non-fireproof carpet from the 1970s, inadequately stapled to wobbly boxes; no 'The Bells Are Up!' signs anywhere; a pretty much empty attendance register; an array of half-empty paint tester pots with the lids left off; and - worst of all - a tray of chocolate-covered Brazil nuts, wide open on the ringing room table without warning labels of any kind! Putting Granser into immediate Special Measures entailed a mountain of emergency paperwork for Bertha, so by the time she got herself over to Frotting, there were only ten minutes available in which to give it the quick once over. All went swimmingly until the one hairy moment when Bertha glanced at one of Hazel's laminated info sheets, which started off by telling her that 'St James the Dismembered has perhaps the most magnificent cock in all of South Shropshire and the Marches...' Time, however, was pressing and Bertha clearly hadn't the inclination to investigate the Child Protection implications of this discovery now, not after such a stressful experience at Granser. Just an advisory note to update any misspelt *documentation was how she dealt with it. Other than that, ticks in every box and all signed off before 9 pm! Top marks to Hazel and Derek there, I think.*

Inspired by the unrivalled beauty and technical perfection of the Frotting bells, Mike has been persuaded to put his addiction worries to one side, to go heavy on the Ibuprofen and Deep Heat for the sake of his shoulders, and just ring himself into an early grave. "You only live once," is his new motto and he is now blissfully back up to two peals per day on average. All of this has been facilitated, incidentally, by Angelique's departure and filing for divorce. She has now hooked up with Bev's ex, Chester Belleau, so rumour has it, and that is all working out a treat. All she has ever wanted, according to Mike, is a man who is always on hand to put up a Laura Ashley pelmet and matching swags, and who will hand over the credit card without complaint. In Chester, she has found her dream man. And Mike's reaction to all this? Unalloyed joy! He has been free to finish off his Battered Sausage, which formed the backbone of our successful long length. Interest in the project has been widespread and enthusiastic throughout the ringing fraternity, and he is now also working away frantically on his Minor methods equivalent: Project Mushy Peas.

Sir Fleet - he did get his knighthood; I didn't just make that up in the throes of my fainting fit! - has continued to court Beverley, turning up for weekly practices at Frotting without fail, and fully rejecting the now-tainted Granser in support of his paramour. (Beverley still refuses to go back there due to simmering resentment on both sides in the wake of the Gaping Wound controversy.) Beverley has appreciated Sir Fleet's loyalty and is starting to believe that, yes, she might not be too ordinary to be loved by a knight of the realm. When he offered her a full-time position through the back door at Granser Sinks, she jumped at it with both hands, and the pair of them couldn't be happier, selling LED-enhanced steam showers by day and ringing themselves silly by night.

The person who has perhaps been the most transformed by the mysterious positive power of the bells is Crispin, dear sweet Crispin. (I secretly want to mother him every time I look at him, although it's pretty clear that he's already had more than enough mothering to last a lifetime.) The self-belief born of turning in the tenor for his first long length has brought out a steely resolve that he never knew he had. The very next day, he finally bit the bullet and told Fleet where he could shove his Granser Sinks. And, as is often the way, slam one door shut and another miraculously opens. For who should be on the phone to Crispin within a week but Lady Boyes, offering him a new role that she had just created as Keeper of the Willey Music. (Workmen had broken through an old wall in the house to discover a gigantic old ballroom filled with dusty harpsichords, ceiling-height mahogany library stacks crammed full of virtually untouched sheet music, alabaster busts of dead composers and a full-size Baroque church organ in need of complete restoration.) He thought all of his Christmases had come at once, and when Lady Boyes continued to explain that the post would be a residential one - he could move out of home! - and that he could share the job and his west wing apartment with a 'special friend' - Dom! - Crispin almost exploded with euphoria. The pair of them are now blissfully ensconced in Willey and, thanks to Dominic's ever-present guiding hand, Crispin's organ has come on in leaps and bounds.

His only problem is Dympna, who has made irritatingly satisfactory progress at Clungefunton. This is thanks in part to a happy accident when, as a contestant on Bargain Hunt, something that needn't be described splatted out onto the auction room floor during her attempt to do the show-closing 'Yes? Yes!' kick. A kindly researcher came to her rescue and, after pulling some strings with friends in high places at Channel 4, he managed to make Dympna's wildest dreams come true… Yes, she was to be given the opportunity to share every last detail of her medical history with Dr Christian on Embarrassing Bodies, along with several million unsuspecting viewers! Dr Christian, whom Dympna says reminded her of her Crispin, was most understanding, and promptly sent her off for an all-expenses-paid bout of gynaecological underpinning. As a result, she has come away with such a magnificently strengthened core that she can now even bong along to Doubles as a more than adequate tenor lady. She can also ring up and down with confidence and can hold her own in Rounds and Call Changes without batting an eyelid. She even has the terminology nailed now, and hasn't referred to standing the bell as 'making bell ends' for months! So, Dympna now makes her own way to Frotting pretty regularly in her Honda Jazz, and Crispin just has to *grin and bear it manfully. At least she never comes anywhere near Willey, much to his relief. She's far too busy logging into daily Zoom yoga sessions (by order of Dr Christian) and volunteering for the Pelvic Crisis telephone helpline.*

And finally, what of Bob? The immaculate Bob, whose thighs would make George Ford weep with envy; who will eat my vegan quiche without complaint; who is making good steady headway towards his ten-thousandth peal; whose Long London is so perfect that it keeps me awake in the middle of the night; whose impeccable touches still send shivers down my spine; who can always put himself right in my Fanybedwell, no matter how messy it gets; who brings me pleasure every second, of every minute, of every day; who never fails to surprise, to delight... What of Bob, you ask? Well, just let me tell you...

Ringer, I married him!

THIS IS ALL!

Also by Carbaretta Bartland

A Short Touch of Bristol

Tintinnalogia II: The Revenge

The Ten Tinkers

The Lost Ring of Fingringhoe

Turn and Face the Strange: Changes on Eight for Beginners

O, for the Love of Lord Rutland!

The Fellowship of the Mini-Ring

Queens at the Back: Crispin's Story

(Available from all good cardboard boxes in the garages of nominated ringing association librarians everywhere)

About the Author

Carbaretta Bartland is the winner of the 2019 Verity Felcher Memorial Award for Campanological Erotica. When she isn't writing international bestsellers, she enjoys travelling the length and breadth of the nation in search of old organs in need of restoration. However, chronic neck pain has prevented her from indulging as much as she would have liked to in recent years. At home in her cottage, she makes adjustable elasticated straps to help ringers avoid the perennial problem of exposing their beer guts at backstroke, and also organises Ladies' Guild jumble sales. She lives in Shropshire with her husband, Johnny, who provides no emotional support whatsoever and spends all of his bloody time on the golf course. She drinks Yorkshire Tea nowadays and smokes Silk Cut Extra Mild, or Lambert & Butler Gold at a push.

Praise for *Her First Long Length*

"Over the course of these 40,320 words, the extent of Carbaretta Bartland's masterful creativity within the field of tintinnalogical romance is sure to amaze, to delight, to stimulate... I only wish I hadn't died three hundred years before having the opportunity to read it."

The ghost of Fabian Stedman (via Zoom séance.)

"No comment..."

The Ringing World

Printed in Great Britain
by Amazon